THE SPIDER:
THE MAD HORDE

THE MAD HORDE

By Grant Stockbridge

ALTUS PRESS • 2019

PUBLISHING HISTORY

"The Mad Horde" originally appeared in the May, 1934 (Vol. 2, No. 4) issue of *The Spider* magazine. Copyright 2019 by Argosy Communications, Inc. All rights reserved.

CHAPTER 1
THE MANIAC KILLS

THE SHORT-WAVE radio beneath the dash of Richard Wentworth's roadster whistled in thin crescendo, and a voice rasped out: "Scout car 2103, go to 567 Crossroads Street. An insane man is in the house. Scout car 2103, go to...."

The dispatcher's voice broke its stereotyped sing-song and grew clipped find hurried.

"... an insane man in the house. WGPK, Cologne Police, Dispatcher Frederick. *Hurry! He's killing someone!*"

Wentworth felt the horror that caught at the throat of that dispatcher, used as he was to the chronicle of a hundred crimes a night. A maniac, killing someone.... A tingle ran down Wentworth's spine. He peered out beneath the pale brows that were part of his disguise and spotted a street sign, white letters showing against an enameled blue field; *Crossroads Street.*

"Stop the car," Wentworth ordered, and Ram Singh, his Hindu servant, swerved to the curb, the powerful motor soundless beneath its sleek, streamlined hood. The night was a smother of darkness upon a suburban street of homes whose windows were yellow oblongs. It was June, but there was no softness in the air. There was heat, sultry as the breath of hell, and on the far horizon sheets of lightning shimmered.

Wentworth listened and felt coldness run like poison through his veins—felt his scalp tingle beneath the close clasp of the

blond wig that concealed his own crisp black locks. To any man it would have been horrible, that cracked hoarse and high-pitched bark and the yammering, senseless howls that followed.

They died out as if the throat that sent them shivering into the night had strangled over the cry and choked it off slowly. The sound itself was terrifying. But to Wentworth it spelt a far more fearful menace. For that cry, blood-chilling and full of an eerie threat, was the howl of a dog gone mad. And Wentworth, driving disguised through an Ohio town, knew that somewhere

THE MAD HORDE

Wolves—dogs—cats—rats—
Vampire bats—all victims
of hydrophobia—spreading
death-dealing havoc.

in this vicinity was a man who had recently purchased five thousand dogs!

"Wait and watch," Wentworth told Ram Singh and sprang to the pavement, his hand sliding to the flat automatic beneath his arm. He waited for the dog to cry again. It did not howl, but another sound tore the night apart—sent Wentworth sprinting down the pavement toward a house whose windows blazed light. That sound, rising high and shrill in the evening silence, tightened Wentworth's heart with dread. It was the cry of a woman in mortal terror, screaming hoarse words of frenzied, pleading protest.

"Do-on't! O-o-o-o-h—God!"

Then silence. Silence in which the swift thudding of Wentworth's feet was like the heartbeats of time. He cut across grass, took four steps to the porch of the house in a single bound, crashed his elbow through the glass panel of the door. Broken fragments glistened on the floor, fragments that contained numbers in gilt and black. 567.

... Go to 567 Crossroads Street, an insane man in the house....

That hurried radio message echoed in Wentworth's ears as he reached through the broken glass, unlatched the door and flung inside. A moment before terror had screamed in the house; now it was still, as still as death. In the hall a lamp with a red shade gave dim light. Beyond a partly closed door, white brilliance blazed. Then Wentworth heard it, a snorting sound that was half like the short bark of a dog, half like a human being breathing.

The partly opened door moved slowly, and a man with massive

shoulders, with a drooping shaggy head, was silhouetted against the light. In his right hand he held a hatchet that was smeared with blood.

The man's chest labored. From his mouth issued the snorting half-bark that was like a worried dog. As he gazed at Wentworth, his jaws began to champ, to snap together like a slavering wolf's. White foam flecked his lips. Wentworth knew those dread symptoms. *The man had hydrophobia!* One scratch from his teeth meant death! The man raised the hatchet with its bloody bit, charged.

WENTWORTH SLID aside like a shadow before an advancing lamp. As the madman blundered past, slashing violently downward with the hatchet, Wentworth slipped a black-jack from his pocket and struck accurately behind the ear. The madman fell, his body twitching horribly. His jaws snapping....

Wentworth darted beyond him into the room of brilliant light. It was a shambles. Two children, a boy often, a girl a few years younger, lay upon the floor, their skulls crushed. No life there. But the woman, her forehead gashed, her golden hair streaked with blood, still breathed.

Snatching out a first-aid kit, Wentworth dropped to his knees beside her. A hypodermic needle shot in its stimulant. His hands moved skillfully as a surgeon's. Bent over its task, his face was keen, the gray-blue eyes alert.

Despite the disguise, the pale brows above his eyes, the straw-yellow hair that bristled upward with Teutonic brusqueness, the square-built forehead and jaw which Wentworth's make-up genius had contrived, the vital strength of the man

5

was apparent. Calm behind those wide-spaced eyes was such a brain as is given mankind only once in a generation, the brain that made him a Master of Men, that inspired the genius-directed Crusades of justice, that had created the Spider.

To his ears as he worked came the whining crescendo of a police siren. He worked on, trying to bring one instant of consciousness to this dying woman, one instant of intelligence during which she might give him some clue to the cause of her husband's hydrophobia. The man Wentworth hunted might well be behind it.

He bent lower over the woman as the first fluttering sigh of returning consciousness stirred her breasts, tautened them against the thin cheapness of her calico house dress. Wentworth waved smelling salts beneath her nose. Footsteps pounded on the porch. The woman jerked as the salts knifed into her nostrils. Her eyes flew open.

"Quickly," said Wentworth, "was your husband ever bitten by a dog or a cat?"

The woman's eyes clouded with pain.

"No!" she gasped.

"Have you called in a strange doctor?"

Wentworth saw in the woman's eyes that he had guessed the truth. But the footsteps now were in the hall.

"Quick! His name!" he ordered.

The woman's lips opened, sound began.

"Hands up, you!" a voice ground out behind Wentworth.

He jerked his head about, eyes blazing. Two police stood with leveled guns.

"Shut up!" Wentworth ordered. He whirled back to the woman, bent close. His hand shot to her throat. There was no pulse. He worked frantically for a few moments, then straightened slowly. The woman was dead. If those police had delayed a half second longer... Wentworth got to his feet, turned toward the men.

"Did you put handcuffs on him?" he demanded. "He'll be coming around in a few seconds, and—"

The guns thrust their muzzles toward him. "Hands up!" one of the police ordered again. The muscles knotted along the ridge of his heavy, outthrust jaw.

Wentworth's blue-gray eyes were like flame. "Fool!" he spat out. "I'm the doctor. Put handcuffs on that man in the hall!"

"There ain't no man in the hall," said the cop stolidly. He swallowed heavily. His face was pale and his eyes shuddered away from the three who were horribly dead upon the floor. "And you're coming along with us! We found the hatchet you used...."

"Is he gone?" Wentworth's tones were excited. "Good Lord, officer, that man has rabies, hydrophobia. He's crazy. He'll go around killing every living thing he meets. Don't you understand?"

THE MEN still stared at him stolidly, the guns unwavering in their hands.

"Get around behind him, Oscar," directed the square-jawed cop. "If he's got a gun, take it."

"You fools!" Wentworth snapped, then caught himself up. There was nothing to be accomplished through argument.

Eventually, he would convince them. But meantime, that madman was loose in the city, that mad dog whose howl had shivered through the air was a constant, horrible menace.

Wentworth's lips opened. From them poured a high-toned cracked bark, a series of senseless, choked howls. The square jaw of the cop dropped open. He retreated a step. Wentworth sprang sideways into the path of the one called Oscar. Oscar threw up his gun with a cry of fright. It was wrenched from his grasp almost before it was raised. A thrust on the throat sent him reeling, strangling backward upon his companion.

Wentworth fired upward. The lights went out. Blackness shut down upon those pitiful, hacked bodies, upon two frightened and dazed police. Wentworth went out a window. A flitting shadow plunged toward him. Lightning flamed across the heavens, glinted on the fearsomely bared teeth of the shadow, a dog that sprang without sound, whose least scratch meant death by torture!

Wentworth hurdled the charging beast. As his feet struck the ground, he whirled and fired. The beast fell, writhing. The menace of the mad dog was eliminated. But the madman was free, his brain numbed by the agony of the disease, goaded by its torturing pain to strike at every living thing that crossed his path…. Wentworth's lips puckered and he sent a wailing, high-pitched whistle into the night. The answer came from three blocks down the blackened street. Wentworth whirled that way, sprinting.

On all sides excited voices were calling back and forth from the closely clustered homes. The shouts of police were hoarse.

Wentworth heard their blundering stumbles in the house. Their white lights stabbed rays about, thrust inquiringly out the window and found the carcass of the mad dog. Wentworth's swift feet left behind the confusion of their search for him. His car whined backward up the street. He sprang to the seat beside Ram Singh.

"A man who left the house just before the police came! Where is he?"

The Hindu's dark face jerked toward Wentworth, his eyes glinting.

"He took a car from the next house, *Sahib.*" His words came in rapid Hindustani. "He drove like a man without his senses toward the highway."

"Follow him," Wentworth ordered, his chest stirring to the rhythm of his swift run. "That man is without his senses. He is mad. God help anyone he meets tonight!"

CHAPTER 2
CASTLE OF GLOOM

THE HISPANIA'S tires moaned as the big car swung from Crossroads Street into the Columbus Road. Ram Singh nailed the accelerator to the floor and presently a spot of red dancing like a fire-fly showed ahead of them on the highway.

The Hispania droned on. The car ahead became defined in the back glow of its own headlights. It was a small coupé. As Wentworth watched, it yawed widely, sidled almost off the highway, then darted with equal vehemence for the opposite side. It continued to zig-zag like that, though its pace was furious.

"Ease off," Wentworth ordered tensely.

He knew what that erratic driving meant. The madman's paroxysm of insanity had passed. He was in the grip of one of those semi-sane interludes of pain when he was stricken with a partial paralysis, but during which his mind was more nearly normal. The man must have some purpose in driving along this road when he persisted despite the pangs of hydrophobia. Was he intent on vengeance, or—?

The last of Cologne's street lights flickered past. The road swooped up and down over rolling hills like a Coney Island switchback. Woods, as black as the storm clouds piling on the horizon, alternated with the sweeping smooth lawns of rich estates. And ever ahead danced that fire-fly tail light.

Sultry wind in his face, Wentworth lounged back into the soft depths of the Hispania's cushions, his mind racing like his roadster's flying wheels. What fearful thing was this that threatened, heralded by a mad dog's cracked and senseless howling?

Wentworth had come west to trail a clever and ruthless criminal named, among other aliases, Douglas Brent. A brief story in *The New York Times* had attracted the ever-alert mind of the Spider. It stated that the Associated Societies for Prevention of Cruelty to Animals had protested against the sale of dogs from the pound—where they were supposed to be destroyed painlessly—to scientists who used them for vivisection. The story had stated that in two weeks the New York pound had sold a thousand dogs.

What experiment could require such vast quantities of dogs? Wentworth, investigating, had discovered that during recent months, five thousand dogs had been sold to one man in Cologne, Ohio. A man who gave the name of Douglas Brent. The description of this man—he had been forced to appear personally to, arrange the unusual transaction—had sent Wentworth racing to his home, had sped him and Ram Singh westward to Cologne.

For the secret, exhaustive files of the Spider, mysterious avenger who devoted his life and vast fortune to checking crime, revealed Douglas Brent as a shrewd and utterly unscrupulous criminal who many times had skated perilously close to the gates of prison, once for a particularly brutal and merciless murder in which an alibi had won him an acquittal. Because his crimes had not menaced the people at large, he never before had warranted the Spider's swift justice. But now, a menace as vast as it was horrible was centering about the sinister figure of this man. How vast, Wentworth still could not fathom, but these things he knew. A dog howled, with hydrophobia gripping its throat. A man, crazy with the disease, had killed his wife and two children, and that man had not been bitten by a rabid animal. He had called in a strange doctor. All these things had happened in a city where a singularly cunning and cruel killer had collected five thousand dogs, the chief breeders of hydrophobia! Was Brent about to loose five thousand mad dogs upon the land to further some criminal plot? Wentworth could

scarcely credit it—and yet the Spider had fought many fiendish plots that hinged on wholesale murder. And the few facts
he had gathered were eloquent of crime and death. That madman
ahead might hold the key....

WHILE HE thought swiftly over his investigation, Wentworth had never taken his eyes from the tail light of the maniac's car ahead. Now he snapped forward in his seat as that
red spot amid the blackness darted to the right, swerved left
and bounced into the air with a crash that echoed resoundingly above the increasing mutter of distant thunder.

Ram Singh sent the Hispania lunging forward. The hot push
of the wind became a hurricane. Then with dry-skidding tires
he snubbed the car to a halt beside the smashed coupé. Wentworth flung from his seat, sprang to the other car's side. It was
empty!

A foot on the running board, he vaulted upward and stood
on the hood which had been rammed into a wall of gray granite.
He could just peer over it into high, close-set trees that stirred
restlessly with the breath of the coming storm. Beneath them
a shrubbery-dressed lawn rolled gently toward the distant cold
lights of a house. Wentworth sent the thin rays of his pocket
flash prodding through the darkness. No trace of the mad killer.
He sprang to the Hispania.

"There's a house on the hill here. Up to it, quickly!"

Ram Singh whirled the roadster, sent it zooming up to iron
gates that were heavily braced between stone pillars. Lights
flooded over the car, two gray-clad men, guns at their sides,
popped out a wicket in the gate and strode forward arrogantly.

"There's a crazy man climbed over the wall," Wentworth shouted at them. "He's loose in the grounds. Phone the house! Search the grounds!" The men stared at him suspiciously. Wentworth leaped from the car, and one guard retreated a pace, hand on his pistol.

"Move!" Wentworth snapped at them. "I trailed this man all the way from Cologne. He killed his wife and two children there, stole a car...."

"Where's the car now?" the second guard demanded, hand also on his gun.

Wentworth murmured a few words to Ram Singh and walked gesturing toward the two men in gray uniform. The eyes of the two were direct and hard beneath the visors of their caps. Their hands were ready on their guns and seconds were precious. He could not delay to argue.

Without warning, the Hispania's motor roared wide open. The eyes of the guards jerked to the car. Their pistols flashed out.

"Hey!"

One strode toward the Hispania. As the guard passed him, Wentworth hooked out an arm and caught him about the neck. Carrying the man before him, he charged the second guard. As he rushed, he wrenched loose his prisoner's gun and pistol-whipped the wrist of the second. He freed the guard, leveled their own guns at the two.

"Hold them," he called to Ram Singh, saw the Hindu's flat black automatic take command of the situation and darted for the wicket in the gate. He found no phone there, plunged on.

"Help!" a guard bellowed behind him. "Robbers!"

WENTWORTH SMILED grimly as he sprinted across rolling green lawns toward the lights on the hill that marked the mansion. Overhead trees tossed in a travail of mounting wind. The heat lightning that had danced upon the horizon had died and a great jagged fork of white fire split the heavens. Thunder clapped on its heels. The shouts of the guards were drowned in the torment of the skies.

Clumps of evergreens and flowering shrubs writhed and bunched like wrestling men. Among them Wentworth's stabbing glances found no trace of the madman. Better to dash to the house and warn the people there. At any second that hulking maniac with his powerful shoulders might crash in.

Blue-white lightning flared again against black clouds, and Wentworth, darting out of clustering woods into the open, saw the house rear before him. Frowning gray walls of granite, with turreted towers loomed like a castle. Nowhere was there any bright light. But dim wraiths of luminance filtered out from windows like arrow slits high in the towers; and through the wide French windows on a raised stone terrace, yellow oblongs of it fell coldly, Wentworth threw a swift glance over the entire front of the wide-flung building. Still no trace of the madman. Wentworth hand-vaulted to the terrace, plunged across it to the French doors and rapped heavily on the panes.

Peering in he could make out people dimly through the curtains, two men seated at ease before a leaping fire upon a stone hearth. At Wentworth's knock, they jerked erect in their chairs, eyes staring toward the door. Lightning flared and thunder made the glass vibrate beneath Wentworth's hands. He knew it outlined him as a black, peering figure. The two snapped to their feet. A gun glinted in the hand of one and they strode toward him.

Wentworth stepped back, thrust the guns he had seized from the guards into his pockets. The door was flung open and the wind rushed in, sending the fire leaping furiously, wrenching at the shade of a floor lamp, snapping curtains on the doors. The man who faced Wentworth, gun in hand, was gray and solid.

"What do you want?" he demanded.

"There's a maniac loose on the grounds," Wentworth told him. "I followed him here from Cologne and he crashed his car and disappeared over the wall."

The man before Wentworth stood unmoving, head thrust slightly forward from squared shoulders. Behind him a taller, slighter man whose head and shoulders drooped, studied. Wentworth too. Abruptly the man with the gun stepped aside.

"Come in where I can see you," he ordered.

Wentworth strode in, closed the door and turned the latch. He threw a quick glance over the room, a huge, high-ceilinged chamber whose stone walls were hung with shields and spears of another age. The place was chill despite the thick rugs upon the floor and the leaping fire. The storm had cut the sultry heat, but this penetrating chill was something inherent in the house, in its huge thick walls of gray stone.

There was no one else in the room, but through arched doors, where roseate light showed black draperies, there came the thin plinking of a piano. Its notes seemed muted by the vast reaches of the house.

Wentworth smiled easily. But there was a taut watchfulness about his eyes. Was the madman bound here for vengeance? Did he blame his tortures on one of these?

"It would be much better," he said calmly to the gray man, "if you called everyone together in one room where the doors could be watched. This man has a homicidal mania, hydrophobia to be precise. He just killed his two children and his wife in Cologne."

"Hydrophobia!" It was a woman's gasp.

WENTWORTH TURNED his head slowly, stared at that arched doorway where the light was roseate. A woman stood there now, a woman in trailing scarlet silk against a draped arras of black. Her hair was black, too. It made her white skin whiter still. She came forward slowly.

"Did you say hydrophobia?" she asked hesitantly.

The square face of the man before Wentworth became firmer, the jaw line more sharply defined. When he spoke his voice was harsh and unmusical.

"Will you tell me now what all this is about?" he demanded.

Wentworth bowed slightly, "I will," he said, "but I'd do it more willingly if everyone were in this room—out of danger."

"The castle is well guarded," said the man impatiently.

Wentworth smiled. "I'm here."

The man started as if he had not before realized the import of Wentworth's presence unannounced, had not realized that he must have evaded his guards.

16

"Your guards were as obtuse as yourself," Wentworth said shortly. "I was forced to circumvent them at the gate so as to, warn you in time. Are you going to—"

He broke off shortly and shouted, "Help! Help! Police!"

In the room beyond, the music stopped with a discordant crash. Servants popped in at another door, and in the draped archway where the woman in scarlet had stood, a pale girl in blue appeared out-lined against the dark clothing of a husky young man whose brown hair straggled an obstinate lock across his forehead.

Wentworth smiled thinly at the man in gray. "Now that all are safely in this room I feel more comfortable about taking time to talk," he said. "My name is Sven Gustafsson," he went on, giving the name he had assumed for the present investigation. "I was driving through Cologne when I heard a woman scream and immediately after that a mad dog howl. You are familiar with the sound that a mad dog makes?"

He paused, eyeing the five people before him and the two men servants who still stood in the doorway beyond the fireplace. Lightning spewed blue-white flame against the French doors, dimming the lights within. Thunder smacked against the walls. The wind made a low whining, then a shriek in the chimney.

The woman in scarlet moved closer to the gray man with the gun, moved closer to the man with the stooped thin, shoulders. Now that she was near, Wentworth saw that her lips were red as bruised cherries, And there were smudges of shadow about black tragic eyes. Her shoulders, bare and warm despite the chill of the gaunt house, made an exquisite line of her throat.

17

Her bold coloring made the stooped man insignificant until he twisted his face toward the door and the harsh direct rays of the lamplight showed the thin-bridged nose, the puckered firmness of a small mouth. Save for that mouth he was not unhandsome.

"Get on with it," the man with the gun said impatiently. His iron gray hair was as close as a steel cap upon his skull, and his face was gray and bitter.

Wentworth told of breaking into the house in Cologne and following the madman after his escape. He made no mention of the police. The girl in blue came closer now, The broad young man with the recalcitrant hair moved like a part of her, behind her with a hand protectingly upon her rounded shoulder. The girl was pale, her hair like sun-warm straw, yellow and gleaming. She was pale, but her lips were red.

"I followed the car till it crashed against your wall. When I reached it, the man was gone." Wentworth waved a hand. "I came to warn you."

The gray man let his gun hang at his side now. "It's easy enough to find out if you're telling the truth," he said.

"Quite," Wentworth nodded. "You can send some men—I would arm them well if I were you—to look at the wreck of the car. It's about two hundred yards south of the main gate. You can call police and ask them what happened at 567 Cross-roads Street in Cologne…."

"What's that address?" The words were snapped at him by the gray man.

Wentworth repeated it, and the blue eyes of the man were

like chips of frozen sapphire. "That's the address of the captain of my guards," he said slowly. "He has been ill for two days, and—"

The flare of lightning was so startlingly brilliant that it stopped his words and pulled all eyes toward the French doors. High and clear, even above the explosive crash of the thunder the screams of the two women knifed the air. Outside those windows, outlined against the dazzling burst of the lightning were the hunched shoulders of a man with a massive, sagging head.

"The maniac!" Wentworth barked out, hand flying to his gun.

The doors sagged, burst inward with a blast like a shotgun, and the man reeled in, his mad, wild eyes roving, lips flecked with white. Wind charged in with him so that he seemed a part of the heaven-ripping storm. Tensing his powerful arms, he advanced toward them!

CHAPTER 3
A MADMAN'S WARNING

WENTWORTH WALKED slowly forward to intercept the man, his gun ready in one hand, blackjack gripped in the other. The gray man's harsh voice rasped out behind him:

"What does this mean, Rusk?"

The maniac's mouth opened, breath barking in his throat. Sounds that were scarcely human came with his harsh breathing, sounds that hinted vaguely at words. Wentworth stood on alert feet just beyond his reach.

"Warn you!" the man's word-sounds phrased. "Warn!"

"Against what?" snapped Wentworth.

"Here, drink this," said a voice at his elbow, and Wentworth heard the gurgle of liquid from a bottle.

"Fool!" Wentworth bit out, whirling. He knocked the bottle across the room,* spun back to the mad-man called Rusk. The maniac had stiffened, head thrown back in torture. His jaws snapped like a dog's and mangled his tongue. Blood spilled from his mouth corners. He reeled backward, hands clutching at his throat. His dragging feet tripped him and he plunged to the rug, writhing in tortured convulsions.

Behind him, Wentworth heard the terrified cries of the women, the confused voices of the others. He dropped on his knees beside the mad-man, careful to keep clear of those plague-laden jaws. Rusk's writhings became a violent threshing… He was dying.

---

* AUTHOR'S NOTE: It is a peculiarity of the advanced stages of hydrophobia that despite an intense craving for drink, it is impossible for the victim to take any liquid. Even the sound of liquid frequently is enough to bring on the violent paroxysms which precipitate spells of madness and which ultimately fall the person afflicted. The snapping of the jaws is part of this muscular reaction, the hoarse breathing a part of the throat and chest paralysis, which also are symptoms of the malady and not, as once was thought, due to a transformation of the human being into something doglike by the strange and horrible disease.

Wentworth snatched out the medicine kit he always carried, thrust a morphine filled needle into an arm he managed to pin down for a moment. Gradually the threshing quieted. Wentworth bent over the man.

"That warning," he said clearly. "What was it?"

His eyes, his powerful will commanded the man. The morphine began to take hold. For an instant, the dying man's gaze cleared. His mouth began to work; sounds squeezed out between his hoarse, terrible breathings, "Warn doctor!"

"What doctor?" Wentworth demanded.

The man writhed, eyes clouding with madness.

"What doctor?" Wentworth bored into him with his icy gaze.

The man's convulsions mounted to a climax, so that his body was inhumanly contorted, then broke into sudden limp stillness.

"Brent!" Rusk whispered clearly. "Brent!"

His chin drooped, his head sagged to the side. His hoarse breathing slowed. Wentworth got to his feet, turned from that tormented body, to the others in the room. The two women had their faces buried on the chests of two men, the tall young man with the sprawling hair and the stoop-shouldered one whose offer of a drink had precipitated this violent paroxysm which was bringing on the man's death.

The gray man still faced him, narrow eyed, lips folded in upon themselves by their compression. Wentworth's thoughts were whirling. This dying man had cried a warning against a Dr. Brent. And Douglas Brent was the ruthless criminal Wentworth was hunting, fearing that he planned to loose hordes of hydrophobic dogs upon the people of the nation!

With the sound of the dying maniac's hoarse breathing still in his ears, visions of horror arose before Wentworth, visions of the hundreds of thousands that, fleeing before the mad hordes, would be bitten and die in writhing torment.

True, the use of Pasteur injections had cut deaths from this dread ailment to a scant hundred a year in the United States, but for that very reason the

A man's scream began and ended in a
choked curse—as he plunge from the tree.

23

danger of this fiendish attack was increased.* Because the disease

* AUTHOR's NOTE: There are a number of ways of preparing the injections which build up immunity to hydrophobia, but all have as their basis the preparation of a weakened virus which is injected at gradually increasing strength. The usual method is to infect rabbits with the disease by means of injection directly into the brain and by passing the germs through a series of animals, using virus each time from the last animal infected, to build up what is known as a "fixed" virus. This virus has a "fixed" incubation period of six to seven days. This process is necessary because of the widely varying incubation period of the "street" virus. After this "fixed" virus is achieved, rabbits are injected with it and allowed to run the full period of the disease up to the last day when they are chloroformed. Their spinal cords then are removed and dried in stoppered bottles, in the bottoms of which potash has been placed. Pasteur's method was to start with injecting emulsions of spinal cord which had been thus dried for fourteen days. The second day spinal cord dried thirteen days would be used, and so on until fourteen injections had been made, the last being of cord, dried only one day. Fourteen days after the final injections, immunity has been built up. The U.S. Pharmocopoeia method is to begin with cord dried eight days. This is the so-called active immunization method and is the basis of almost all anti-rabic injection, though varying methods of weakening the virus are employed, including heat, gastric juice, bile, etc After the cord has been weakened by the desired number of days of drying, it may be kept at this fixed strength by immersion in glycerine. But glycerine will preserve the cord only 30 days. Then new preparations must be made.

There is another method of injection which was developed by Babes and Lepp, later by Tizzoni and Centanni, which is called "passive" immuni-

was comparatively rare and the serum of an intensely perishable nature, few laboratories prepared it and they kept only small quantities. That meant that if this monster loosed his hordes suddenly and over a wide area there would not be enough of the serum in the nation—in the entire world—to save those whose torn flesh would admit the fearful germs of madness and death.

But what could possibly be the purpose of such wholesale destruction? Wentworth could only guess. But this much is apparent: The guard who had died had been struck down for some definite reason—apparently by an injection of the virus by a Dr. Brent. And the victim had apparently believed that the threat affected his master also, affected this gray, challenging man before him.

SLOWLY THE gray man put away his gun. "I thank you, Mr. Gustafsson," he said heavily. "I appreciate the great lengths to which you went to warn me." He ordered a butler to call an ambulance for his guard, sent another to bring Ram Singh to the house. He offered his hand to Wentworth. "My name is

---

zation. In this method instead of injecting the virus of the disease, the scientists inject a serum from an immunized animal. This method has had some success and has been preferred by some because only two injections a few days apart are necessary and because the preparation may be preserved longer than the perishable Pasteur cords. However, it is the Pasteur method which is now used almost to the exclusion of the other systems of both active and passive immunization, because this method has had the widest tests and the widest success.

Berthold Healy," he said, his voice as harsh and unyielding as the solid palm that met Wentworth's.

When they had left the chamber of horror for the music room beyond, he introduced the others in turn. "My wife," he said, and the woman in scarlet turned a pale face.

"My daughter—"

The girl in blue nodded, still shrinking against the chest of the hulking young giant behind her.

"My daughter's fiancé, Jack Collins." The young giant nodded, his lips set, and the straggling lock of hair sprawled across his forehead. He tossed it back with a jerk of his head.

"And Heinrich Scarlet."

The stooped man came forward and gripped Wentworth's hand strongly, his handsomely strong face apologetic.

"I have to apologize for offering that poor man a drink," he said softly. "I didn't realize… I forgot for the moment… hydrophobia."

Wentworth nodded affably. "Quite all right," he said, "the natural thing to do."

He turned toward Healy.

"May I have a few words in private with you?" he asked.

Healy nodded his compact, gray head, gestured with a restrained arm toward another door which revealed book-lined walls when he touched a light button. Wentworth walked in with him. He heard subdued voices rise behind them.

The young man called Collins drawled to the girl, "Do you feel like playin' any moah, Go'geous? It might take yoah mind off…."

Scarlet offered Mrs. Healy a drink.

Even into the library, the chill dampness of the building penetrated. The flashes of lightning outside the room's single high window were almost continuous now. As Healy waved Wentworth to a seat, an especially violent crash of thunder broke the back of the clouds and sent the rain down in a washing flood across the window. Healy dropped into a lounge chair and was absorbed into the shadows of its wings. Wentworth sat opposite him beside the black hearth and offered his platinum cigarette case, lighted up when Healy refused.

"I want to tell you in advance," Wentworth said, snapping out his lighter, "that it looks very much as if this attack on your guard was actually directed at yourself. The fact that Rusk came here to warn you is pretty evident of that. I hold certain powers from the federal government for investigation and I was on the trail of a man named Brent when I came here. Brent was the name Rusk gasped just before he died. I tell you this because I want to ask certain questions."

WENTWORTH SAW the shadows shift in the depths of the chair and knew that Healy had nodded his head.

"What business are you in, Mr. Healy?"

The man rasped his throat harshly. His voice came sharply out of the dark.

"I'm tied up with a number of industries," he said. He jerked to his feet, stood a moment, then started pacing up and down with short, striding legs. "My biggest holdings are in steel. Steel town near here is my biggest plant. Six or seven thousand men and their families live there."

Wentworth's pulse quickened. An attack of rabid dogs against an industrial town could cripple the operation of that factory!

"Have you any other such towns?" Wentworth asked softly.

Healy halted his pounding stride up and down the room, stopped and stared down at Wentworth. His feet were braced, straddling out before the black hearth, his arms locked behind him. With his short, corpulent figure and his large, square-cut head, with its close-cut hair like a steel cap, he might have been Napoleon in modern garb.

"Yes," he said in his unmusical, harsh voice. "I have a number of such towns. The people are happier that way and I have a firmer grasp upon the workers. They are less apt to become disrupted by radicals. I have cotton-mill towns in North Carolina; I have communities of workers on wheat plantations in the west, this steel town, a couple of mines…."

"You are very wealthy then?" Wentworth asked, the false square brows of Sven Gustafsson frowning.

Healy stood immovably rigid before the hearth. "Not immensely," he said heavily. "My holdings are extensive, but not very rich." He chopped off his sentence. "Would you mind telling me where all this is pointing to?"

Wentworth stood. "Just this," he said. "A man named Brent has bought more than five thousand dogs. If he gave those dogs hydrophobia and releases them on one of your industrial towns, wouldn't you pay handsomely to save the others?"

Healy's head jerked up. Breath hissed between his teeth. "The damned scoundrel!" he grated out. "Would any man release mad dogs on women and children just for money?"

Wentworth's mouth twisted thinly. "Men have killed before this for money," he said.

"But mad dogs!"

Mad dogs! Distantly as he spoke, through the even wash of the rain, the retreating thunder of the storm, came a cracked, high-pitched bark, a senseless yammering of howls that clenched Wentworth's fists at his sides! The sound jerked Healy about in his tracks—to stare panicked eyes at the black bulb of the single high window. As they stared, distant white lightning burned and something hunched and furry was outlined against the panes!

Healy's hand flew to the gun in his pocket. He sent lead crashing through the window. A cat yowled thinly like a suffering child, and the hunched, furry thing was gone. Healy spun back toward Wentworth. His face was drawn. Excited voice's from the next room screamed questions.

"In God's name, what is happening?" Healy demanded of Wentworth.

Wentworth smiled thinly. "Rusk warned you," he said. He spun toward the door. "I'll be back. I want to find that mad dog that howled." He paused a moment. "Do you know a national guard commander near here?"

Healy jerked a nod, frowning. "General Lansing. Brigadier General Francis Lansing at Saginal. He comes here some times."

Wentworth nodded and went out.

THE FOUR in the music room were hurrying toward the library as Wentworth strode out. The women stared with frightened eyes. The two men started forward, then Healy showed

in the doorway, and they fell back. Wentworth hurried on, past two men in white who were lifting the still-unconscious madman to a stretcher. He passed out into the high, vaulted hallway where Ram Singh, imperturbable behind folded arms, awaited him.

Out into the sheeting rain, Wentworth strode. The Hispania was not in sight, and he raced to the cover of the bowing trees, Ram Singh at his heels. Once more, reedily through the night, came the insane howling of a dog. But it was no longer a single cry. It had become only one of a muffled chorus of mad yelps. Wentworth reached the wall. Ram Singh crouched, hands linked between bent knees. A quick step, a heave and Wentworth was atop the wall.

Once more the thin, senseless howling, this time almost at hand. No slinking black forms ran blindly along the road; no threatening horde of madness loomed, but the yellowish lights of a large truck sped toward him, the heavy rain like slanting crystal rods across its headlights. It droned past, and abruptly, Wentworth knew why the howls had seemed muffled. They came from inside of that truck. *A load of mad dogs was being transported to be loosed upon an unsuspecting countryside!*

Wentworth sprang down from the wall.

"Quickly, Ram Singh, the car!"

Ram Singh darted away. Wentworth headed for the gate. A rustling sounded above his head, and he flung aside, as a horrid, yowling scream tore downward and claws struck into the shoulder of his coat. Teeth grated as they gnashed in the brim of his hat. It was a cat, and that thin, hoarse cry meant it was mad with the fearful madness of death, *a cat which had hydrophobia!"*

CHAPTER 4
HORDE OF DOOM

WENTWORTH KNEW that if that mad cat's teeth struck into his throat or face, he would have small chance of escaping the horrid death of madness, for the germs attack first the brain, and wounds in the throat and head are nearly always fatal. If he attempted to seize the hydrophobic animal with his hands, he was certain to be lacerated.

He knew these things without conscious thought, and he acted as swiftly as the knowledge flashed across his mind. He flung to the ground, rolling, felt for and found a water puddle, rolled the clawing cat into it.

He heard Ram Singh dart close.

"Stand clear, Ram Singh!" he snapped, but the Hindu ignored the command.

Wentworth felt the cat ripped from his shoulder, heard its body strike suddenly against a tree as it was flung savagely aside. He sprang up, snatched out a small pocket flashlight and turned it upon Ram Singh. A glint from the tree above caught his eye. His automatic leaped to his hand, belched leaden death.

A man's scream began and ended in a choked curse, and a man's body plunged downward and thumped upon the wet ground. He flopped over on his back and Wentworth spotted the bullet hole in his forehead. He paid no further attention to the man, ignored the distant shouts of Healy's guards and made a hurried examination of Ram Singh. The Hindu's right wrist bore the toothmarks of the mad cat!

Wentworth took Ram Singh's keen-edged knife and gashed out the flesh about the wound, then he tugged out his medical kit. At a sign from him, the Hindu bared his abdomen and into the flesh, Wentworth shot the contents of a hypodermic syringe.

"Get the car quickly," he told the Hindu and wordlessly his servant turned away.

Wentworth whirled to the body of the man he had slain, stared down at the face by the white light of his hand torch. The face was strange to him, a lowering, dark countenance. Wentworth drew out a cigarette lighter and pressed its base on the brow of the man who had attempted to murder him with a hydrophobic cat.

When he had taken the lighter away, a red spot glowed on the man's forehead, a red spot that had hairy, ugly legs.

It was Wentworth's calling card of death—*the seal of the Spider!*

He restored the lighter to his pocket, seized the body and with a single heave of his broad shoulders, lifted it at arm's length above his head and tossed it over the wall to the road. That would warn the criminals that justice stalked them! He ran then to the gate of the grounds, found the two guards he had disarmed, waiting there with hard-gripped rifles. When they identified Wentworth, they scowled, but did not bar his way. They had had their orders from Healy.

Headlights flashed down the road, and the Hispania skated to a stop. Wentworth flung in.

"To the left," he ordered. "There's a closed truck we must trail."

The Hispania swished out onto the rain-drenched road, laid its belly to the pavement. In two hundred yards it was doing seventy miles an hour.

Water dripped from Wentworth's clothes and from Ram Singh. Blood dripped, too from the gash in the Hindu's wrist.

But neither man heeded it. Wentworth knew he had cut no important veins. The bleeding would help prevent infection. The Hindu did not know this. But he trusted his master.

AFTER TEN miles of roaring speed, the tail lights of the truck came in view on the black, twisting road.

"Slow," said Wentworth.

It was possible the blow was not to be struck yet, that the mad animals were merely being transported to a convenient center of operations. If that was the case, Wentworth had no wish to prevent the truck from reaching its goal. By following it he might find the lair of the criminal leader himself!

The Hispania crested a hill and in the valley far below lights were haloed by dwindling rain, the lights of a town. *Washington Courthouse*, the road signs read. The roadster closed up on the truck. If a man made a move to open it and loose the plague upon the people, Wentworth would shoot him down.

They descended toward the town, jounced over railroad tracks.

The truck pushed on. As they turned left into the main street of the village, Wentworth turned to Ram Singh.

"Burn that wound with strong nitric acid or gunpowder," he said. "It will help insure against infection." He drew out his medical kit, put a fresh charge into the hypodermic needle and handed it to Ram Singh. "Tomorrow, inject this into your abdomen as you saw me do.

"Stop at the next corner. Call the surgeon general's office at Washington in my name, and tell them it is imperative that anti-rabic serum be generated at full speed and that large quantities be shipped to Ohio. Tell them that there is going to be an outbreak of hydrophobia here such as the world has never before known!

"Phone General Francis Lansing at Saginal and tell him, for me, that a plague of mad dogs threatens and he is to prepare for a call. Tell him to call Berthold Healy for particulars."

The Hispania slowed, Ram Singh dropped out and Wentworth instantly took up the pursuit behind the wheel. Lucky for Ram Singh, he thought, that setting upon the trail of dogs, Wentworth had thought to supply himself with a dosage of anti-rabic serum,* the passive variety which was rarely used, but which required only two injections. He had carried only that single double dose, but if it saved Ram Singh, he was repaid for the risk he must run from now on, unequipped with a guarantee against the dread hydrophobia.

---

* AUTHOR'S NOTE: This was the Ceteri method described in a previous footnote.

MILE AFTER mile through the night, the plague-bearing truck droned northward; and ever behind it Wentworth tooled the sleek Hispania. The rain had ceased now. The white of drying cement began to spot the black wetness of the road. Wentworth turned his mind to the man behind this impending horror. Back in Cologne, he must check up on this Dr. Brent whose visit had preceded the death of Healy's guard.

That was a queer thing, that death. Why did the criminals, if they intended to attack one of Healy's industrial towns, begin with the murder of one of Healy's *home* guards? And why were mad cats loosed about the grounds of the estate? Killing the goose even before it laid the first golden egg seemed a trifle absurd.

Abruptly Wentworth straightened behind the sensitive wheel on which his hands rested lightly. The truck was swooping down a long grade, and in the valley below the patterned lights of another, larger town were laid out with geometrical precision. Off to the right there was a glimmer of gray light along the horizon, the first herald of dawn. Its dim radiance faintly illumined a line of fat chimneys, tall along the southern edge of the town. The truck swooped toward it like a diving eagle. The Hispania's motor deepened its roar....

Here, Wentworth realized at once, was an industrial town. He saw that a crossroads signboard flashing past spelled out *Eatonville*, and he frowned. A steel town, right enough but not Healy's. Grimly, Wentworth crowded the truck. To loose that captive horde of rabid dogs upon the town, men must open the back of the truck. When they did....

His left hand light upon the wheel, Wentworth dipped into his pockets, drew out the two weapons he had taken from Healy's guards, and laid them upon the seat. He gripped his own automatic in his right hand. The mad race down the grade ended in a dwindling drone of powerful engines. The truck turned right and threaded a way between tall brick buildings protected by fences topped with strands of barbed wire. Guards paced within.

Wentworth frowned again. Of what use would mad dogs be in an attack against such a place? Give the industrialists a few hours notice, and they would have every man, woman and child behind such fences with sharpshooters in impregnable towers ready to fell any mad dog that came near. Mad dogs? Yes, but couldn't hydrophobic cats wriggle through? And if this damnable fiend could use cats and dogs, why not other animals? Why not rats and mice which could filter through a still finer mesh of defensive wire? Why not….

Wentworth cursed and spurted as the truck whirled a corner at high speed and shot eastward. For hours the wailings, and howlings of the mad horde had been silenced. Now the blood-chilling chorus of doom sounded again.

With frantic speed Wentworth wove in and out among the red-walled factories, shot clear of the tangle and sped among wide-lawned suburban streets. Lights burned in windows now as men prepared to go to the mills. A woman opened a door and stooped for a bottle of milk. The truck spun a corner and sloughed to a stop.

Wentworth flung his Hispania broadside. With grimly watching eyes he crouched forward, two guns ready in his hands. The first man who opened a door... then, without warning, the back of the truck popped open, swinging from hinges at its bottom! It dropped to the street, forming a perfect gangway—a gangway for the Mad Horde of doom!

The inside of the truck was a stygian cavern, full of a thousand unseeable horrors. For an instant there was neither sound nor motion. Then a single dog thrust from the blackness into the light. Its lower jaw hung laxly and flecks of white clung viscously to lips and fangs. There was red madness in its eyes.

The bark of Wentworth's gun was swift as thought. The dog sprang vaultingly out into the air and crumpled in the street. As if Wentworth's shot had been a signal, a half dozen more menacing heads thrust into the light. His guns spat again and again, but now there was a stampede of the Mad Horde. Dog after dog he tumbled dead in the street.

But others poured out behind them, reached the ground in a single bound and trotted on stiffly mechanical legs off into the half darkness amid the homes with their unsuspecting victims.

GUNS BLAZED now form the black interior of the truck. Wentworth crouched behind the bulletproof sides of the roadster, tooled it so the windshield protected him. He fired only at the plague spreaders. The men could wait.

Still they poured from the huge truck, dogs and cats, huge sewer rats, white laboratory rats and mice. Truly a horde of horror. A scratch from the teeth of any one of those beasts, and a man would die in writhing agony. And these animals would attack on sight any living thing they met! Other hundreds of dogs and cats and vermin would become infected and help to pass on the mortal madness. For months, the virus would spread....

Wentworth churned among the mad horde with the heavy wheels of his car. A dog with drooling jaws sprang upward at his leveled gun hand. He jerked down the muzzle, fired directly into that yawning mouth. Its dying body slammed against the side of the car.

A cat hooked its claws over the door, Its snarling mouth a red threat of death. Wentworth's lead hurled it to the street. Pale faces showed at the windows of nearby homes now. A man flung wide a door and strode out, a hulking fellow, with suspender straps over his chest-bulged red undershirt. A rifle was in his hands.

A half dozen dogs swerved in their soundless fury and hurled at him. Two he shot. A third got past his rifle, and the man struck with his fist. The animal buried his teeth in it. Two more dogs struck him. The man cursed, lashing with his rifle. A dog got past him, and within the house a woman screamed.

All about Wentworth's car lay the carcasses of mad animals, but scores had escaped. The truck, its tail door slowly rising into place again, lurched forward. Not a man had showed himself.

The Hispania surged in its wake, but three blocks farther on Wentworth hurled about a corner, jerked to a halt before a cottage and raced to its door. His frenzied beating brought no response from within. He snatched a lockpick from a compact kit of tools he carried always strapped beneath his arm. In seconds the door yielded and he plunged into the dark hallway, found a phone and called police.

"This is a federal investigator," he spoke with crisp syllables. "A criminal has just turned loose scores of mad dogs, cats and rats upon the city… Yes, hydrophobia… Get every exterminator you can busy eliminating them, and phone Washington for anti-rabic serum. Yes, hydrophobia. I don't know who did it."

He slammed up the receiver and darted to the door. He jerked it open, and a policeman leveled a revolver at him.

"Hands up!" The man ordered. "I saw you break into this house."

"But, officer," Wentworth stepped forward a pace.

"Keep back!"

Wentworth's left hand brushed the revolver's barrel aside. It jerked with the explosion of its discharge, and lead slammed through the door behind him with a crashing of glass. Then the policeman went backward and down from a right to the jaw, and Wentworth was sprinting toward his car.

Police sirens moaned in the distance, crescendoed to a wail as a squad car with a half dozen men clinging to it rounded the corner. Wentworth reached his car, slapped a hand to the door, then snatched it away as a furred fury flung at him from within, a rat with gnashing teeth. Wentworth's gun flew to his hand. A bullet smashed the mad rodent's head, hurled its kicking body to the floor. A jerk at the door, and once more Wentworth halted. The bullet that had wiped out this new menace, a rat undoubtedly planted there by the criminals he pursued, had smashed through the ignition switch of the Hispania! Not a chance to start it.

The squad car skidded to a halt, nose jammed against the Hispania's front bumper. Even if Wentworth had been able to start it, he could not have escaped now. Men spilled from the squad car, riot and machine guns glinting in the double glare of the autos' head lights.

Two men sprang toward Wentworth, sawed-off repeating shot-guns leveled.

"One step," the leader spat out. "And you're a dead man!"

One step, yet Wentworth could not wait. While he stood there, a captive of police guns, the murderers who had loosed their fearful hordes upon the city were fleeing. While he attempted to explain, they would put miles between them and the Spider. Miles that meant defeat!

Wentworth stepped to the side of his car.

"Halt!" the cop ordered again. "One step, I said, and—" He lifted the gun, his eyes cold behind the wide black muzzle—a muzzle that could blast a hole like a dinner plate in a man's body....

CHAPTER 5
THE DEATH-HEAD BRAND

WENTWORTH HAD his back to the Hispania. He slid his left hand behind him into the pocket on the door, fingered out two glass tubes that nestled there. Luckily his abandonment of the car could not incriminate Richard

Wentworth. The motor numbers had been stripped from it, and the license plates were in the name of Sven Gustafsson. He could leave that all right, if he could escape the police.

He stared into the threatening muzzle of the riot gun while other officers crowded close behind the man who held it. A sub-machine gun was held low at the hip by a second policeman.

"One step is a mighty small thing to kill a man for," Wentworth said calmly. "Don't you think so?"

He took one step backward.

He saw the policeman's eyes narrow, and he dived behind the car, as the blast of the shotgun ripped open the night. Its buckshot peppered the back of the Hispania but Wentworth's leap had been lightning fast. He rolled toward the far side of the car, tossing the glass tubes at the feet of the police by lobbing them over the Hispania's low top.

The shotgun blasted again. The machine gun stuttered, drumming lead against the armor of the roadster. Thin gray gas spiraled upward from the broken tubes of glass. The man with the riot gun reeled backward, choking. The machine gun stammered its leaden hail again.

"Stop it, you fool," a man gasped. "You'll kill some of us."

Coughing, choking, eyes streaming from the tear gas Wentworth had loosened upon them, the police scattered to escape the fumes. Behind the Hispania, Wentworth sprang toward the squad car. The driver had fled with the rest. Under the Spider's skilled hands, the car leaped backward, checked and, whirling on moaning tires, whizzed up the avenue. Banging guns were as futile as the strangled shouts of the gassed police.

Within three minutes Wentworth was out of the town, the way cleared by his moaning siren, and was racing southward again, back along the road over which he had trailed the truck of the Mad Horde.

The truck was unburdened now. It would make fast time, but that long grade out of Eatonville would slow it, and…. Bellowing into the first gradient on the climb, Wentworth peered ahead through the dawn, red now with the first light of the sun, and saw

its rays glint upon a crawling truck near the crest. The squad car roared wide open. It was a third of the way up when the truck dipped from sight at the top. When it crested the rise, the truck was a mile away, rounding a curve like a schooner heeling to the wind.

Wentworth nailed the accelerator to the floor. The speedometer needle wavered at sixty and crept upward as the momentum of the roaring green car mounted. Past sixty-five, and upward. The red truck was swaying wildly. A coupé skittered from its path and poised on the brink of a ravine, toppled slowly. A man leaped out and shook an infuriated fist as the machine rolled downward. The squad car zipped past at seventy, its siren shrieking once.

On a downgrade, the truck held its own, then, braking for a turn, twisted its rear from side to side violently. It swung, half broadside into the curve, flashed out of sight. Moments later, even above the bellow of his own motor, Wentworth heard a rending, fearful crash. He cut the gas, kicked the brake, and went around the curve at fifty. The railing of a bridge was smashed through. The truck lay on its side twenty feet below, its rear out of sight in a narrow, deep creek that streamed muddy clouds over its splintered red fragments. Wentworth, braking savagely, jerked his eyes to the woods that crept close to the road and spotted moving branches. He threw the squad car to the left of the highway, flung out while it still rolled and readied the woods in a bound. The running footsteps of three men sounded plainly on the rain-softened earth. He dived into the woods, reloading the automatic clenched in his fist. Trees were thick and scrub growth choked the way. Visibility was less than fifty feet. The ground became hard, the trail of pounding foot-steps dimmer. Wentworth halted, listening, heard a furious threshing through underbrush ahead.

He plunged on, ducking under down swooping limbs, weaving between wrist-thick saplings whose switches slashed his face with a sting like nettles. The growth became thicker, but still the crashing ahead led him on. Beneath his feet, the earth slanted downward. He ran faster, ducking briar vines. The grade grew steeper so that he skidded on his heels to slow his descent. Abruptly, he bent double, dived headlong and hooked an arm about a small tree.

A huge gray beast hurtled over the spot where he had stood. Long white fangs snapping, it whirled with silent fury.
SPINNING ABOUT the tree with the momentum of his dive, Wentworth snapped a shot into the animal's head, sent it

threshing to the earth. He regained his feet and crouched, steadying himself with a hand lightly against the tree. Ten feet away shrubbery crashed violently and two more of the gray beasts charged with hanging heads, and slavering jaws. They were wolves, mad wolves, and upon their foreheads were branded human skulls, the symbol of death!

The evil import of those branded skulls, the proof this attack by mad wolves was a trap of the criminals he trailed, might have unnerved a lesser man, laid him a stunned and helpless victim before the slashing fangs of these savage beasts. But Wentworth's gun hand was steady, his eye as unfailing as ever. Twice his automatic spoke. And a bullet, smashed through the center of each death's-head brand.

Wentworth flung himself aside from the wolves' dying slashes. He screamed horribly with his throat wide open, beat about in the shrubbery with his left arm. But his right hand gripped the gun ready. He kept on screaming, let his cries grow weaker.

The wolves were dead now, lying stretched out stiffly on the earth. But all animal victims of hydrophobia are silent when they attack, silent when they are wounded. Their silence gave no warning to the man who, sneaking through the shrubbery, thrust out to make sure of the victim's death. He stared with mouth agape at Wentworth, straightening from the covert where he crouched.

Wentworth, a grim smile on his mouth, waited until the man's surprise changed to fear, until desperately he jerked up a gun. Then he drilled the man through the heart. He bounded past him and on through the woods. Fifty yards more and he saw sky between the far trunks of trees and seconds later burst out onto another road. But its far curves were empty. A quick search of the earth revealed the footsteps of three men beside the deep tire tracks of a car. His quarry had escaped.

Wentworth sped back to the body of the man he had slain. A swift search of his pockets revealed no clue to his identity, nothing to indicate where headquarters of the gang might be. Wentworth's mouth was straight and hard. The gangsters had spread their havoc, left their death-dealing hordes to kill and had shaken off pursuit. Obviously, this escape passage through the woods had been well planned, the man planted there to cover the retreat after the truck had been wrecked.

Wentworth's hand slid to his cigarette lighter. He stooped over the dead man, over the slain wolves and on the forehead of each, in the midst of the death's-head brand, he imprinted the menacing red seal of the Spider.

The Horde Master's men had escaped, but not unscathed. Back there by Healy's home lay the body of one; here was another beside three of their foul servitors, the mad wolves. The Horde Master would know that the Spider was on the trail!

The sound of a roaring motor that died into a mutter jerked Wentworth's head about. It came from the direction of the squad car. Police had arrived. Then the Spider must be on his way.

AS HE strode silently southward through the woodland, Wentworth's hands were deftly at work. The yellow wig was removed with the false blond brows and, dampened with an inflammable fluid from the cigarette lighter, flared into an unrecognizable charred mass beside the Spider's swift path.

First putty, then transfiguring plates of thin, hard rubber came from mouth and nostrils and forehead, and now it was Richard Wentworth himself that stole through the thickets with such soundless efficiency, his lean jaw firm with determination, the gray blue of his eyes cold as ice.

The vital strength of the man was at once apparent, even to a casual glance. Striding along, he skillfully applied black grease paint that gave him a stubble of beard, putty that gave him a broken nose. A scar disfigured an eyebrow. Gone now was Richard Wentworth, wealthy clubman, dabbler in criminology, dilettante of the arts. The man who slouched through the underbrush, his torn coat and mussy trousers burred with woods briars, was a tramp of the road.

The tramp eluded the clumsy police cordons—Wentworth was a trained woodsman; these others were city men—and made his way at last back to Cologne. There, no longer a tramp, but still with his broken-nosed face, he called his fiancée, Nita Van Sloan, on long distance and asked her to drive West, bringing at least one dose of the anti-rabic serum for herself. She was to try to gain friendly entrance to the Healy home. Among her friends some undoubtedly could give letters of introduction. Wentworth knew that Sven Gustafsson had been revealed as the Spider, that his entree at the Castle had been destroyed.

He asked Nita to phone Professor Brownlee and ask him to hasten West, where he was to make every effort to develop some

47

means of killing the Mad Hordes. "I suggest a gas strong enough to kill animals, too weak to affect humans," he said.

Then Wentworth called Washington, got in touch with the surgeon general's office and identified himself.

"It is essential," he told them, "that even more serum than I ordered through Ram Singh be shipped here."

The surgeon general interrupted him. "I have not heard from Ram Singh!"

"You are positive?" Wentworth snapped out the words, hands tense on the phone.

The surgeon general told him the only order for serum had come from Eatonville and that a plane was speeding the equipment there. There could be no doubt about it. Ram Singh had not communicated with Washington!

That could mean only one thing. The faithful Hindu had been prevented by force from fulfilling his task. Either he was a captive of the Horde Master, or he was—dead. Wentworth's mouth shut in a grim line.

"If you want to get more supplies nearer at hand," the surgeon general was saying, "there is a laboratory at Columbus, the Aachen, which has some of the virus on hand."

Wentworth hung up and stood staring at the white wall above the hotel telephone he was using. Ram Singh in the power of the criminals! The thin white scar upon his right temple began to throb, red and angry. If they harmed that faithful fellow.... But there were even more serious connotations of his capture. If Brent were alert to the possibilities, he might trace the Hindu through Washington and find that he was attached to Wentworth, learn that Wentworth and the Spider *were* one!

A curse grated between his teeth. It would be fatal now to have the hordes of the criminals loosed upon himself. He must maintain his incognito, continue to battle in secret. He would rescue Ram Singh and smash this gang, but first he must speed to the Aachen laboratory at Columbus. It must throw all its energies into producing the anti-rabic serum, He caught up the phone again and waited five minutes in grim-faced impatience while the operator tried to raise the laboratory. Finally she reported the line, "Out of order."

Out of order! Wentworth knew what that meant!

"Operator, see that the police are sent to investigate the reason for that wire being out of order. I am positive that criminals are responsible," he snapped. He slammed up the receiver, hurried to the car he had rented since loss of his Hispania and sent it hurtling through the midday traffic to the Cologne airport.

Yes, he knew what that report meant. But God alone knew if he would be in time to avert this new infamy of the Master of the Horde! Not content with striking down thousands with the most dread disease of the ages, Wentworth feared the criminals now were planning to take away the last hope of the doomed wretches they had infected.

The Horde Master was *attacking the laboratory that produced the serum!*

CHAPTER 6
GUARD THE LABORATORIES

A T THE airport, Wentworth chartered a plane and, springing to the controls himself, sent it skimming from earth, splitting the air toward Columbus. It was eighty miles to the laboratory. Wentworth, straining the motor to the last notch, made it in thirty minutes.

As he swooped above the low-lying laboratory building seeking a landing, he saw men run from it with backward firing guns, saw them leap into a car and race away at top speed. Wentworth threw the plane into a steep bank and whirled in pursuit. Leveling off, he gripped the stick between his knees, jerked two vials from the kit beneath his arm, poured their contents into a silver flask, which he first emptied of the brandy it contained.

Darting low over the racing car, he hurled the flask accurately into the road. It flashed down past the nose of the car, striking almost beneath the engine. It burst with a flashing roar of sound, a spear-like blossoming of white and red flame. The front of the car was thrust straight up into the air. It plunged in a twisting somersault into the ditch.*

---

* AUTHOR'S NOTE: I have tried many times to learn the secret of these two fluids which were another of the many inventions which Professor Brownlee contrived for the Spider, for whom he had an undying and unwavering affection. As nearly as I could make out from the somewhat technical analysis that Mr. Wentworth once gave me, the professor had contrived

Like an echo of that ripping concussion, a cyclonic explosion tore out behind Wentworth. He felt the plane stagger and slide off on the right wing. Desperately, he fought the controls in a maelstrom of freak air currents. One glance backward told him what he had guessed. There had been another, greater explosion than the one caused by the hurling flask. The laboratory had been blown into fragments! Bits of masonry and torn bodies hurtled through the air. Wentworth clenched his teeth, battling the crazy controls. The plane was fluttering within a hundred feet of the earth. He threw the stick forward, jerked the ship into a sharp dive.

Rudder surfaces had been torn, and the ailerons of one wing flapped loosely, but the speed of his dive gave him the beginning of control, and he managed to wheel the ship into a side slip. He wrenched about again and took the ground at eighty miles an hour. Sixty was normal landing speed. The plane struck on the wheels alone, bounced violently.

Off balance with its broken aileron, it dug a wing into the earth, cartwheeled and buried its engine in the mud. Half-dazed, Wentworth freed himself from the belt, and struggled clear. Gun in hand, he sped in a stumbling run toward the wreck of

to split trinitrototuolene into two component and harmless parts. This made it possible for the Spider, despite his occasionally strenuous physical encounters, to carry the two vials of liquid in has kit without fear that a chance blow might set them off and blow him to bits. Yet, when the two were mixed, he had at his command one of the most powerful explosives known to man.

the car he had blasted from the road with his improvised bomb. He darted out into the road, then stopped dead in his tracks.

High, leaping flames wrapped the ruin of the car. The black billowing smoke betrayed that the gasoline tank had burst. No clue there. And the laboratory building had been blown to bits! There would be none there.

The fiendish deliberation with which this criminal worked stunned Wentworth afresh. The laboratories could not turn out the serum swiftly enough to save more than a tenth of those he had stricken with his dread plague, but he removed even that possibility. He had destroyed the laboratory which made the serum! It would be weeks, months before the valuable laboratory equipment, the virus built to "fixed" strength through long intensification in laboratory animals, could be replaced.

Good God! Were they striking at all laboratories? The government must be warned. Guards must be set about them. Otherwise the entire nation would lie helpless before the assault of this ruthless criminal.

Wentworth whirled to race to a phone, a telegraph station, anything to spread the warning. He whirled and froze, hands at his side. Two police had crept upon him while the roar of the flames had hidden the noise of their approach. They stood with leveled pistols. A police car rocketed up the road, stopped with a squealing skid of its tires, and two more men sprang out with drawn guns.

One of the first police began to curse Wentworth with a slow, cold venom.

"You louse!" he snarled. "We saw you in that plane bombing

the laboratory! You've killed half a hundred men." He bit out a curse. "Hell, you lousy, murdering…" He aimed his pistol. There was murder in his eyes.

CHAPTER 7
AMBUSH IN THE SKY

FOR AN instant the life of the policeman leveling his pistol at Wentworth hung in the balance. Through the Spider's mind raced the necessity of his own escape, not for his own sake, but for the humanity he ceaselessly defended. The Spider had never killed police in his countless crusades, never intended to. They, like himself, fought for the people. But this gun in a crazed man's hand imperiled the entire crusade…. Wentworth was poised for swift action when the policeman's companion struck up his gun hand, sent the lead whistling harmlessly into the air.

"Fool!" he said hoarsely. "You almost killed him!"

"I meant to!" the other raged. "He bombed the laboratory and Sarah…."

Ah, the policeman was motivated by personal vengeance. This was no vast cosmic rage that stirred him to kill in the name of justice. Wentworth, his face very grave, moved toward the four police slowly.

"Listen," he said, wagging his head with a vehemence they would understand. "I didn't have a thing to do with that laboratory. I was in the plane and saw the men in that car over there run out of it shooting back at the laboratory. I dropped a bomb on their auto and spilled it over the ditch. That's all I had to do with it. You can look in the auto and you'll find their guns, and…."

"Stand still," the second policeman ordered."

Wentworth gesticulated with his hands. "I'm telling you the truth. I'm a government agent and I was coming here to warn the laboratory. The same gang that spread hydrophobia in Eatonville bombed this place because it makes the serum that they use to prevent hydrophobia. You can call Washington…."

The policeman who had attempted to kill Wentworth stepped forward and struck at him with his gun. "You louse, you killed Sarah!" His face was white and tightly drawn. Tears ran from his eyes. "You louse!" He struck at Wentworth again and each time his gun swished harmlessly past a ducking head.

Wentworth made no move to strike back at the policeman, made no move to seize the opportunity this man's closeness offered for escape. Wentworth's nimbleness infuriated the policeman. He leveled his pistol again.

"Take this nut away," Wentworth warned, "or I'm going to knock him for a loop."

"Oh, you will, you louse!" The policeman squeezed the trigger again at almost point-blank range. His tightening eyes had betrayed his intention and the lead burned the air past Wentworth's side. He stepped close, his fists battering. The cop went down. Wentworth sprang back, both hands raised.

"I had to do it," he said rapidly. "He was going to kill me."

Two more policemen were coming at him slowly now, their leveled guns ready.

"He ought to," spat one. "Killing his daughter that-a-way." The amiability went from Wentworth's face, left it lean and hard. His eyes had ugly lights in their depths.

"Permit me to remind you," he bit out, "that the execution of justice is not in your hands. You are police, hired by the people to arrest suspects, not to lynch them."

The police continued to advance from two sides with their weapons ready. The third officer stood directly in front of Wentworth at a distance, and the other two were careful not to come between him and their quarry. All three were silent.

"I'm warning you once more," Wentworth said deliberately. "I'm a government agent. Take me to your superiors and I'll present my credentials. Touch me at your risk."

"Yeah, you're a government agent," a policeman jeered.

Wentworth smiled into the man's face.

"Incomprehensible as that may seem to you," he said quietly, "that is precisely what I am."

"Then let's see your papers."

Wentworth shook his head slowly. "I present those only to the commissioner himself."

"He's faking," barked the first policeman. "Let's rush him." He raised his gun like a club.

WENTWORTH TOOK a cigarette case from his pocket, tucked a white tube between his lips. He looked upward beneath his brows at the policeman as he lifted flame toward the cigarette.

The cop's lower lip thrust out. He took two strides forward with clubbed gun ready.

Wentworth lifted his head, puffed through the cigarette. No smoke rose from its tip, nothing seemed to happen, but the policeman checked, took another blundering step forward and, a surprised look on his face, crumpled to the earth. There was a tiny drop of blood on his cheek.

The Spider bent his head again over the cigarette lighter, ignoring the crumpled policeman, jerked up his head again. Once more he puffed through the cigarette, and this time the sun glinted on a tiny sliver of steel flying through the air, a flying sliver that was too swift for the man at whom it sped to dodge. It caught him beneath the ear and, instantly paralyzed, he too, fell.

Stupidly the third officer had stared while his companions were dropped by the Spider's narcotized darts, blown through a tiny pipette thrust through an ordinary cigarette. The fall of the second officer seemed to snap him from the paralysis of his amazement. He snapped a shot at Wentworth. Crouching forward, he walked in on him, gun belching lead.

The first bullet had sped wide, thanks to Wentworth's split-second reflexes, his ability to dodge like a flick of light. There was no time to insert a third dart in the cigarette under cover of appearing to light it. He snatched out his automatic, and the bullet whanged against the policeman's lead-vomiting revolver.

The man gripped his numbed wrist, stared into Wentworth's set face—and took the third narcotic dart in the throat. The Spider raced to the wreck of the automobile he had bombed, seeking some clue to the origin of these men, some way to trace them to their headquarters. Even the license plates of the car were unreadable, melted out of all shape by the blast furnace heat of the gasoline blaze.

Wentworth, his lips twisted thinly, put his ugly, menacing seal upon the paint-stripped and still hot door of the car, then strode off across the fields.

THE HORROR of the laboratory bombing was all about him. Fragments of masonry and metal were scattered like waste paper over the ground. And there were the dead, men and women and parts of men and women. In the fork of a tree, a girl's nude body was wedged. Her hair was black and stirred faintly in the warm wind. Wentworth strode on, his eyes burning in a dead white face. He could not help the dead, but their dead lips cried aloud for vengeance!

On a parallel highway three-quarters of a mile away, he found a phone in a garage and called Washington, warning the surgeon general to guard other laboratories, advising that they radio a warning to the serum plane and send a convoy of attack ships.

The surgeon general's voice was acid over the wire. "I'm afraid your warning on the laboratories comes too late. Our own here has been blown up. We're checking on others. The plane will be warned."

Wentworth whirled from the phone, paid a garage attendant to race with him to the city, where, his disguise altered once more, he was able to rent a plane although narrow-eyed police examined every person intent on leaving the city.

Despite the fierce need for haste, he moved with deliberate calmness, chatting a moment with the policeman on guard about the horror of the laboratory blast. He climbed leisurely into the cockpit, waved a hand and sent the ship sky-rocketing. He did not spiral for height, but slanted off in a long climb toward Eatonville.

Deliberation dropped from him. He gripped the stick with a rigid hand. His eyes swept the skies feverishly. That plane-load of the Pasteur injections spelled life for the hundreds of those the plague had touched in Eatonville. If the criminals managed to strike that down, too, the chances were there would not be a single dose left this side of the Atlantic Ocean!

L'Institut Pasteur, of France, was rushing three thousand sets of injections on the *Atlantica*, he had learned from Washington. Within five days the ship would dock at New York. But it would then be too late to save many of those stricken. And still the Spider was without a clue to the fiends behind this fearful plague.

Their purpose was still not clear, though their intention to attack industrial towns had been at once apparent to Wentworth. Thanks to his warning, all such towns now were erecting a mesh of steel fences, setting up powerful flood-lights and turning night into day for their expert marksmen. These methods would keep out the dogs and wolves, with the death's head branded upon their fore-heads. It might keep out the cats. Exterminators already were combating the horde of rats and mice loosed by the criminals.

These defenses might suffice when they were completed, but those high, strong fences took time. And meanwhile the hordes could range at will among the helpless thousands of the industrial towns, snapping with paws whose slightest scratch meant death to the innocent men and women and children who were the pawns in this hell-bred plot.

Now the patterned streets of Eatonville rose on the horizon, nestling amid the circle of green hills. The ribbon of the road over which Wentworth had roared in pursuit of the fleeing truck was choked with cars. All their hoods pointed away from Eatonville. Wentworth's mouth was a straight, hard line. Panic laughed its shrill senseless laughter in those streets, the laughter that turned men's blood to water. And here panic took the guise of a wolf with a death's head burned upon its skull, a wolf with foam-flecked, snapping jaws and a cracked crazy howl that was like a maniac laughing....

Wentworth whirled the plane into a steep-climbing spiral, scanning the heavens behind him. Distantly he saw a vague dot that momentarily enlarged. He jerked wide the throttle, hurled the vibrating ship at peak speed toward that spot. Gradually it developed a web-like line to either side. That line thickened into a wing.

Off to the north and to the west, other groups of dots became visible now. Those would be army warriors sent to protect the serum plane. Wentworth held the stick back. The motor labored, but he gained altitude. There were low-hanging clouds that could hide a squadron of enemy planes. If he could get between those clouds and the serum ship... *What was that!*

Tearing from those clouds, splitting the air in an almost vertical dive directly toward the serum ship, Wentworth spotted another ship. He gripped his automatic, the only weapon he carried, and fought to get one more notch on the throttle. Already his craft was traveling at wing-trembling speed. His helpless eyes, watching the tableau ahead, detected a, flickering wisp of flame behind the propeller of the down-swooping plane. It had loosed machine guns on the serum ship!

CHAPTER 8
DEATH IN THE SKIES

THE DEFENSELESS serum ship swerved frantically to dodge those death belching machine guns. It jerked into a side-slip. The diving killer of the skies altered his course and followed inexorably, machine guns still coughing their death message. Through an erratic barrel-roll, a power dive, the plane pursued. No amount of flying skill or daring, it seemed, could save the ambushed serum ship.

The attacking plane was swifter, more dexterous. Easily it followed the writhing, stumbling efforts of the unarmed and heavier serum ship to escape. The end came in the midst of a rudder-kicking, barrel-rolling dive. The tracer bullets smoked home into the cockpit, and the serum plane staggered, zoomed and stood on its tail, pitched off and plunged downward in a screaming tail-spin.

Black smoke blossomed as it bored toward the earth; black smoke, then a vicious red fang of flame that turned into a flapping tongue that licked the whole underside of the ship.

Wentworth's lips twisted into a thin, snarling line. The serum plane was doomed, but the ship that had struck it down, if it escaped these on-sweeping squadrons, should lead the Spider's fangs to the kill. He wrenched on the stick, sent his plane vaulting into the protecting cloud banks above, himself shrouded in silver mist. Skimming on upward to the sun-drenched tops of the clouds, Wentworth began a slow, wide circling. The pirate craft would undoubtedly seek this protection. Hedge-hopping would be the only other recourse and with those armadas of the air converging, low altitude would be dangerous.

He had scarcely completed a single circle of his grim patrol when the killer vaulted above the cotton-wool cloud tops and, tearing through the crests of those gentle waves, streaked southward, where still thicker bands of mist were piling up. There was a distant dark threat of storm and preliminary lightnings stabbed the murk with flame. Wentworth dived into the clouds and compass-steered southward also.

Now and again, he hurdled upward in a porpoise leap that spotted the ship ahead, and concealed his pursuit again instantly. Of the army armadas there was no trace. Either they had been shaken off by the swift flight to the clouds or they prowled below, futilely. Once, far off, Wentworth spotted a circling ship, but it was soon left behind by their swift southward rush.

For five minutes now, Wentworth did not spy upon his quarry. Then he eased back on the stick, ripped upward out of the mist, and, with a cry in his throat, hurled it back into the obscurity of the clouds again. As he had thrust into view, he had spotted the pirate craft directly overhead. It had dived instantly, twin death flames flickering at the muzzles of its machine guns. And Wentworth's only weapon was an automatic pistol!

RICHARD
WENTWORTH

Yet Wentworth did not flee the attack. After that single necessary dive, he spun the plane southward once more under the protecting shield of the clouds. He cut his motor and, straining his ears against the drum-deadening beat of the engine, made out the hornet buzz of the other plane slashing through the mists behind him. He gunned the motor, and bucked upward to clear the fouled spark plugs his moment's idling had cost him. Minutes later, the sweet, rhythmic beat once more restored, he thrust into the open again, skimmed the tops of the cloud waves.

For the moment, the upper air was clear, but only for an instant. The pirate plane zipped upward in an Immelman, whirled—and once more its guns coughed. The Spider's lips began to smile, and it was a smile that meant death. All hope was lost now of trailing this ship to the lair of the Horde Master, but the Spider would exact vengeance for the wrecking of the serum ship, the doom of the thousands which its fall heralded. With a steady hand he yanked his belts to see that they held securely, then thrust the stick all the way forward. He held it like that, spun downward in that most perilous of all air maneuvers, an outside loop!

INSTEAD OF whirling with the bottom of the plane outermost so that the force of the whirl thrust him more deeply into the cockpit, he would somersault with the cockpit outermost, with his body straining to yank free of the restraining belts, with the blood driven to his head by terrific centrifugal force, pounding numbly in his temples. The pirate ship ripped toward him, tracer bullets burning their smoke-streaming path directly overhead.

As Wentworth's ship vanished once more in the cloud bank on a maneuver that the killer could not dream would be attempted, the pirate ship swooped upward again, vaulted into

an ordinary loop and swept back, waiting for its victim to show again. That hovering craft was like on eagle with outstretched claws ready to grasp a helpless pigeon, armed only with a feeble beak.

The pirate ship reached the bottom of its loop and Wentworth, head buzzing with the pressure of blood, dangling by the one strap that still held after that death-defying outward loop, swept up on his tail, scant yards away. A kick at the rudder and for a fleeting breath of time, the two ships raced side by side. The startled face of the pirate pilot swung about, mouth agape, an arm flung up unconsciously to shield himself from the leveled gun in the fist of the Spider.

Spewing out the entire clip of bullets, Wentworth fanned the cockpit of the other ship with lead. Then he slammed forward the stick, dived into the tops of the clouds and kicked into an Immelmann, sweeping back past the pirate plane on its other flank. In that swift passage, he had flipped out the empty clip of his gun, jammed in another with his right hand. Now, gripping the stick with his knees, he yanked a cartridge into the chamber and was ready.

The two ships zipped past at a combined speed of better than three hundred miles an hour. Wentworth attempted no shot. It would have been futile. He saw the pilot hunched forward in his cockpit, then he had darted past, flung into a vertical bank and was upon, the pirate's tail.

The killer was maneuvering weakly. His plane was boring downward toward the clouds with the pilot crouched in his pit. Wentworth knew he had scored a hit. He threw the stick forward, yanked the throttle wide and swept on his prey in a whining power dive. The killer twisted his head about, flung up a hand as Wentworth once more swept past with his automatic blasting, then the clouds swallowed both.

It was like a plunge from a brightly lighted room into midnight. The soft gray billows of the clouds folded about them and Wentworth was alone in a world of swirling silvery mists. He eased the throttle, checking the furious pace of his plunge, and pulled out of the dive just as his plane burst through the lower margin of the clouds into the dull, gray light of a shadowed world.

The pirate ship was below him, its tail whirling in the fatal nose-down corkscrew of a spin. On and on the pirate ship plunged and Wentworth heard in imagination the banshee-screaming of its taut wires, wailing for the pilot's death. The plane struck nose-on in the edge of a meadow, bounced upward, spattering fragments over the landscape, and collapsed on a crushed side.

After that nothing stirred there, except a flock of crows rising in mucous flight and flapping heavily to nearby dead trees. They peered bright-eyed at the wreck, took to slow wings again as another ship glided to a landing and a man crossed to the wreck, hauled out a dead man and pressed something that glittered to his forehead.

If they flapped near later, scanning that wreckage with their insatiable curiosity, they must have wondered at the sprawling, hairy-legged spot of red upon the forehead of the dead man—*the Spider's warning seal!*

CHAPTER 9
THE HORDES STRIKE

TAKING OFF from the meadow where he had sent the Plague Master's aerial killer crashing to his death, Wentworth swept at mounting speed toward Cologne. He had been forced by the pressure of events to turn aside from his quest there for Ram Singh. And every trail he had since followed had ended in death and the seal of the Spider. If only he could find some trace of Ram Singh, perhaps rescue his faithful servant, he would have a definite clue to the Plague Master and the whereabouts of his headquarters. In Cologne, too, was the trail of the mysterious Dr. Brent.

Those two slight leads, tracing the movements of two men; one abducted or slain; the other undoubtedly seeking in every way possible to conceal himself, were the only clues Wentworth had. And the land lay helpless beneath the assaults of the Mad Hordes of doom. These were the thoughts that raced through Wentworth's mind as he sped back toward Cologne, weary with the ceaseless battle.

As he flew along, he completed with his deft fingers the hurried disguise he had assumed before renting this plane, the disguise of one Patrick O'Roone, a sandy-haired Irishman with a slightly comic, pug-nosed face. His brows, too, were sandy, and a mustache of the same shade bristled upon his lip. His right eye developed a squint, and a gold crown upon an eye tooth complete the picture of the man who set down the plane upon the flying field at Cologne.

Patrick O'Roone was a jocular, robust man, but there were lines of weariness around his eyes, for whatever Patrick O'Roone had been doing in his imitable Irish way for the last forty-eight hours, his creator, the Spider, had been dashing furiously in pursuit of the Horde Master, had battled for his own life and the lives of thousands in the air and on earth and had four times imprinted his dread red seal as a warning to the Underworld.

The Wentworth that was Patrick O'Roone joked with the mechanics at the field, got them to notify the Columbus concern from whom he had chartered the plane that he would be needing it for a few days more and strode with the toe-treading lightness of an athlete to a taxi.

As he was sped through the streets, blossoming with the lights of early dusk, Wentworth saw police stationed in pairs, saw that people moved hurriedly, with eyes fearfully intent upon the shadows. His pug-nosed face remained half humorous, his right eye squinted as in amusement, but his heart began to pound high and thuddingly in his throat in the tempo of anger. He knew what those actions meant. The fate of Eatonville was not enough to cause them. The Horde Master had struck some new blow!

The taxi hit a red traffic light and lounged up to the white stop line at Main Street. Wentworth signaled a newsboy, hoarse from shouting extras, and bought copies of the *Herald* and the *Cologne News-Leader*. He held the *Herald* toward the rays of a street light.

23 SERUM LABORATORIES BOMBED

Wentworth caught that headline, saw the word "Healy" in a second streamer, then the taxi inched up on the changing light and, getting the signal, slithered into Main.

The papers must wait. He stuffed them into the wide pocket of his coat.... Wentworth would not have done that, but Patrick O'Roone was slightly sloppy as to dress.... He halted the taxi at a corner, paid off, and from nearby shops bought a Gladstone bag and some haberdashery. These things were necessary, because police would trace him through the plane wrecked at the laboratory, which they would know had carried the Spider.

His purchases were all a part of his new identity.

ANOTHER TAXI dropped him beneath the rococo marquis of the Cologne Vanderbilt hotel. He registered again. It would have taken a clever student of handwriting to have detected that the Patrick O'Roone who sprawled big letters along a line was the same man who, a broken-nosed, slightly disreputable figure, had signed earlier this same day in a crabbed, uneducated hand that matched well with his appearance.

Once in his room, Wentworth began a detailed study of the newspapers. The second biggest story, topped only by the laboratory disasters which had killed nearly a thousand persons, was the news that Berthold Healy had narrowly escaped death at the hands of a maniac guard who had already murdered his wife and two children. A small smile twisted Wentworth's mouth. The *Herald* had a nice gift of dramatization. He read on.

In a moment of consciousness, as he was dying, Rusk apparently realized the enormity of his crimes and tried to make amends by whispering the name of the men responsible for them. Police said the name was kept secret, although thorough investigation had revealed no trace of the man named. He was supposed to have been a physician, police reported.

Wentworth squinted the right eye of Patrick O'Roone. Police already had hunted this "Dr. Brent" then—had done that piece of work for the Spider. But why had anyone at Healy's done anything so ridiculous as to give that clue to local policemen when Wentworth had identified himself as a federal investigator?

Further reading told him what he had half forgotten. The identity that he had given Healy had been revealed as that of the Spider. Small wonder then, that they had called in police! Still Wentworth skimmed on through the story. Scarlet had done the talking for the household.

There were pictures of Mrs. Healy—her name was Sybil, and the daughter, Doris. Tomorrow, he hoped, Nita Van Sloan would contrive an entrance there, and then he would once more have an inside contact. Meanwhile, this Dr. Brent....

The Horde Master had blasted every laboratory in the country that conceivably could be used for the manufacture of the serum. The government had arranged for shipment of a huge supply, three thousand treatments, by L'lnstitut Pasteur on the *Atlantica*, the world's fastest steamer. Within five days that would arrive and, the government assured the people, there would then still be ample time to treat those who had been infected by the bites of hydrophobic animals.

Fourteen days to several months, according to the location of the wound, was the incubation period of the disease, and long before the malady could strike, the Pasteur injections would have built up immunity. Thus the government!

The Eatonville stories stated that twenty persons already had been stricken with hydrophobia, despite cauterizing treatment at the time of the attack. No known form of the disease had ever struck so quickly, doctors stated. They were skeptical, insisting that infection must have taken place some time previously without the knowledge of the victim. But no evidence of such previous infection had been disclosed.

WENTWORTH'S HANDS, gripping the newspaper, were white with strain. Not only had these fiends loosed a horrible disease upon the country and destroyed all means of combating that ailment, but they had developed a virus which brought on that dread plague within thirty-six hours. Even if the immunizing injections were at hand, they would be useless against this new form of rabies, for immunity was not developed until fourteen days after the injection!

He threw the papers savagely to the floor. Rest was not for the Spider, though the gaunt lines of fatigue were beginning to tauten his face and his eyes were sunken with weariness. He must act swiftly.

He strode to the phone, called Adjutant General Lansing and identified himself. He told him that troops undoubtedly would be needed shortly to defend cities against the hordes and made certain suggestions for defense. The general's voice was brisk and agreeable. He thought the suggestions excellent....

Then Wentworth turned to the task of finding Ram Singh. He had been reasonably sure until now that the injection he had given the Hindu would have successfully immunized him to the disease. The news from Eatonville made that doubtful now. Cauterizing within twenty hours after the wound usually prevented rabies, but this new and speedy virus upset all medical information.

He began his search with the hospitals and the morgue, tried police last, but all inquiries were futile. It would be necessary to go to the town of Washington Courthouse, where he had dropped Ram Singh, to trace him.

First, while he was in Cologne, the trail of Dr. Brent must be investigated. Even if the police had worked over the ground, there remained the chance that the Spider might succeed where they had failed. And the trail of Dr. Brent would lead as surely to Ram Singh, Wentworth was convinced, as if he followed the Hindu himself.

He tested his automatic, thrust extra clips of bullets into his pockets and strode out of the Cologne-Vanderbilt and along the evening-darkened streets. A taxi took him to Crossroads Street where first the plague had struck.

Wentworth already had ascertained that the shipment of dogs had not been to any specific address, but to the station itself, where it had been called for. There were no more shipments of dogs to be traced. The broadcast alarm which Wentworth had requested through Washington for the man known to New York police under the alias of Douglas Brent had borne no fruit. There had been no trace of the man for months past. Yet Wentworth knew that in some way Healy's guard, Rusk, had run across a doctor named Brent and had had reason to suspect that the doctor was implicated in a plot against Berthold Healy.

No one was alive in the Rusk family to be questioned. Wentworth walked up a white cement path that bisected the neat green lawn of Rusk's next door neighbor. A woman with a child beside her made a porch swing creak rustily. A man had his chair tilted back, his feet upon the railing. Wentworth took off his hat, flashed the broad smile of Patrick O'Roone upon them.

"I'm looking for Dan Rusk who lives around here somewhere," he said. "Can you tell me where to find him?"

The man took a stubby pipe from between his teeth and spat over the railing.

"Yeah," he said.

"Where?"

"In hell!"

Wentworth allowed his smile to grow uncertain. "I'm afraid I don't understand."

"Dan Rusk is dead," the man said, and put his pipe back between his teeth.

Wentworth shook his head heavily, dug out of his pocket a briar pipe. He stuffed it with an emphatic thumb. "Well, that's the way it goes," he said slowly. "We're here today and gone tomorrow."

The man with his feet on the rail watched approvingly as Wentworth lighted up the blackened pipe. He spat again. "You said it," he declared. "Only I wouldn't like to go the way Dan Rusk did."

IT TOOK a half hour of patient roundabout talking, but ultimately Wentworth learned that it had been this man's wife who had given Dr. Brent's name to Dan Rusk's wife when his stomach began to bother him, and she had done it because a friend of hers had told her how this same Dr. Brent had cured her husband's stomach trouble just overnight.

"But how," asked Wentworth, "did you get hold of this Dr. Brent?" He grinned his infectious gold-toothed smile. "I might get a stomach ache some day myself."

The woman got up from the porch swing, went in the house and returned with a slip of paper on which a telephone number had been penciled. "This woman gave me the doctor's phone number," she explained, "just in case we ever had need of him. She was a real nice lady."

Wentworth traced the phone number and found it was located in an office which had been vacated the previous day, although the rent had been paid for an entire month. The superintendent of the building gave dubious assent to a search. The room was bare of letters and file. Apparently, its sole use had been the telephone placed squarely in the center of the desk.

Wentworth lifted the blotter. Under it lay two yellowed newspaper clippings. One concerned hydrophobia and listed all the laboratories that manufactured the serum. The other was a personality sketch of Berthold Healy with a large stipple drawing reproducing perfectly the square-cut heaviness of the face. Patrick O'Roone, watched by the superintendent, squinted his right eye. The name of the paper was the *Eatonville Press*. The story listed all Healy's holdings.

Wentworth made notes of Healy's holdings and left the clippings. He searched vainly for fingerprints and thanked the superintendent. Ten minutes later, he was on the wing with his propeller churning the night air toward Eatonville.

He sent the plane into a slow glide toward the air field on its western flank and the purple glow of its flood lights fanned out across its level green. Wentworth spotted the swiveling wind arrow with its guttering torches, set the plane down and taxied to the hangars. He gave swift directions for disposal of his ship, ordered that it be kept ready for an immediate take-off and strode toward the two waiting taxis, a hundred yards nearer the administration building.

A sedan spun around a corner of the building, halted before the door. A man climbed out and hurried in. Wentworth saw these things as he paced on toward a taxi, but took no especial notice. From the hangar behind, a man in dungarees ran out calling, "Mr. O'Roone! A message for you, Mr. O'Roone!"

Wentworth did not wait to turn his head. He hurled himself toward the taxis at top speed, high knees flung in a fierce sprint. Out of the corner of his eyes, he saw the sedan dart toward him as the single man who had alighted ran black from the building, pointing toward Wentworth. The sedan's engine whined in second gear, jolting over the rough terrain.

"Taxi," Wentworth shouted. "To me!"

A taxi driver leaned out, saw the sedan's charge and spun his taxi into motion away from Wentworth. The second cab followed suit. Either those two had been bought in by the enemy or they feared to interfere.

Wentworth's lips twisted beneath the sandy brush of his mustache. His swift glance about found no help and no cover. He was in the midst of a wide expanse of open field. The hangars behind? Long before he could dive to their shelter the sedan would have run him down, or the guns of the men would have blasted him into bloody death. The car was between him and the administration building. There was no other cover.

The gears of the charging sedan crashed into high. Straight at him it bored, blazing white headlights shining full upon his racing form. If they were holding their fire, for a moment, it was only to make more sure of his death.

Wentworth's thin grin became a snarl. Death he did not fear. He was prepared always for that eventuality. But his death now would mean triumph for the criminal forces this merciless Dr. Brent commanded. Police had not detected the faint trail which led from a next-door neighbor to an empty office.

That empty office had obviously been watched. They'd spotted Patrick O'Roone and sent their killers to wait for him in Eatonville with ready guns!

CHAPTER 10
A DYING MAN TALKS

WENTWORTH THREW all his superb strength into a headlong sprint. He fairly flew over the earth in a terrific burst of speed. And yet he was racing toward open fields, dashing toward a level stretch of land where he could the more easily be mowed down. In the car the gangsters chuckled. Like everyone else when death threatened, this man had lost his head. The sedan was doing sixty now, plunging like a greyhound, like a sentient beast bent on destruction of its prey. Now it was only a hundred and fifty feet away, now only a hundred. The gangsters' braced for the shock of the impact.

In that instant, Wentworth did an amazing thing, a thing no other man would have had the courage to do. In mid-stride, he dug his feet into the earth and spun to face the blazing headlights, then sprinted to meet the on-rushing death!

Brakes squealed an instant, and the headlights slowing in their charge as the driver unconsciously stepped on the pedal. Then the motor roared again and the lights plunged forward. Steel glinted in Wentworth's right hand. Fifty feet from those dazzling beacons of death, he halted and fired twice. The lights crashed out. Wentworth hurled himself to one side. He checked dead with sliding feet, then flung flat to the earth, as a whining hail of bullets spewed over his head.

It was over in a split-fraction of a second. Wentworth rolled, threw up his gun and pumped bullets after the sedan as it zipped past. A bullet for the right rear tire, one for the left rear, two to make sure the gas tank was ripped open. He threw another at the right rear tire, snapped out the clip and, reloading, sprinted away from the car whose leaping rear light attested the accuracy of Wentworth's tire shots.

A police roadster flung around the corner of the administration building, missed Wentworth but spotted the erratic tail light and bellowed after it with its siren shrieking.

Wentworth had five one hundred dollar bills in his hand when he plunged through the hangar door.

"Quick!" he shouted. "Whose motorcycle? Five hundred for it!"

A mechanic came toward him on slow feet.

"Quickly, man!" Wentworth shouted. "I'm going to get those damned gangsters if it's the last thing I do."

The mechanic jumped at that, his last doubt vanishing under Wentworth's urgent words. He thrust keys into Wentworth's hands, snatched the money and started fumbling for his registration card. Before he could get his hand into his pocket, Wentworth had whirled the motorcycle, jerked it in gear and was pushing it at a dead run toward the door. Under the powerful urge of his rush, the motor blasted out like a machine gun. He vaulted to the saddle and cometed into the dark with twin headlights blazing.

Above the rattle of his own exhaust, he heard the coughing cackle-of a machine gun. The police car's headlights were stationary at the edge of the field, its top down, its two occupants battling. But the flicker of the machine gun's death flame came from the sedan, and the crouching forms of the two policemen stiffened in death. Four men sprang to the police car, their figures black against the fan of the headlights, and the roadster wrenched toward the road.

Wentworth cut his headlights, felt the motorcycle buck like a wild horse between his knees, swerved from the unevenness of the field to the concrete road that bordered it, and roared blindly, in the wake of the fugitive roadster. The Ford beat him to the highway by a hundred yards, screamed its dry skidding tires about the curve and streaked off across the southern boundary of the city, toward that hill road that sloped up from Eatonville.

WENTWORTH LEANED into the curve, saw once more the scarlet dance of the machine gun's muzzle flame. He slammed the motorcycle frantically to the left of the highway, succeeded in avoiding the leaden blast which swept back down the road. His lights were off. But it was only a question of minutes before that searching machine gun sprayed its leaden death through the right section of night air and dumped him, riddled and lifeless, into the roadside ditch.

Once more, smiling grimly, Wentworth drew his gun. Picking out the driver's head among those outlined against the reflected glow of the stolen police roadster's headlights, he emptied his automatic with slow-spaced shots.

Frightened shouts zipped back to him on the air, whipped from the mouths of the men in the speeding car.

The machine yawed wildly. Its tail light seemed to spurt backward toward Wentworth as its dwindling speed narrowed the distance. He cut his own pace, reloading. The Ford swerved wildly again, headed straight across the road. Two tires lifted and it did two barrel rolls and landed upside down, wheels spinning idly in the air.

Wentworth flicked on his two headlights and spilled them over the shambles. Two bodies sprawled in the road. Two others hung from the car. He skidded the motorcycle to a halt, kicked the back-wheel prop down and strode to view the dead. Motors

"Where are your headquarters?" Wentworth demanded sharply.

racketed over at the airport. He must make haste. Swiftly he sifted the contents of his victim's pockets without results. Three of the men were dead and upon their foreheads Wentworth affixed his scarlet Spider seal. The fourth still breathed hoarsely.

The road behind was alive with lights. Autos raced toward him. He caught the fourth man under the arms, tossed him to his shoulder and ran to his motorcycle. He seated the man with his feet outthrust over the handle bars, his unconscious shoulders sagging against Wentworth's chest, and spurted off up the road while ambulance bells and the wail of police sirens lagged far behind. Across the southern edge of town and up the long grade of the highway the motorcycle shot like a skyrocket. Here the road was empty of traffic—Eatonville was a nearly deserted city since the plague had struck—and, his lights out, he followed the concrete ribbon easily by its white glimmer beneath the stars.

After ten minutes without sign of pursuit, Wentworth switched on his lights and jounced across a roadside ditch into a wood lane. When the thick green growth had hidden him from the highway, he jacked up the rear of the motorcycle again and spilled his captive to the ground beneath its glaring lights. He knelt beside him and explored his injuries with swift, wise fingers. The man's chest was crushed. Death was certain. Wentworth's face was hard as rock. If he were merciful, he would let this man, die in coma. If he were merciful—a short laugh escaped the Spider's lips. The Horde Master had not been merciful!

Wentworth took smelling salts from his emergency first-aid kit, shot adrenaline into the crushed chest near the heart.

Groans from the dying criminal, weak groans, then flickering eyelids and consciousness. Wentworth slid into place over his eye-teeth two long glistening fangs of celluloid, stripped off the red mustache and slid on a mask. Thus the underworld knew the Spider and feared him. This face, with lips snarling from menacing white fangs, he thrust into the light above the dying man.

The man's death-heavy lids flared wide. A gasp cut into his sobbing breaths. Before that staring face, Wentworth thrust his hand with the ring of the Spider, a black ring with a sprawling red spider upon it.

"God!" The man panted. "*You!*"

The flat laughter of the Spider mocked him. "I bring you death," he said coldly. "Torture and death. There is still life in you. I can make you—" Wentworth thrust forward the snarling, masked face with the glistening fangs. "I can make you *suffer!*"

"No!" gasped the man. "No!"

Wentworth slid a glittering knife into the narrow cone of light, advanced it toward his prisoner's face. Groans came from the dying man; groans but no words.

"You can save yourself," said Wentworth softly. "A few words from you, and you may die in peace. I have morphine to let you die in peace!"

The man's chest heaved horribly. Blood dribbled from his mouth corner. He tossed his head and groaned. "What…."

"Where are your headquarters?" Wentworth demanded sharply.

The man's head rolled in new agony. Wentworth slid a hypodermic needle into view. "Peace," he said, "peace in this needle!"

The head became still, the eyes focused on the needle. Gaze unwavering on the syringe, the man began to move his lips. Wentworth bent close, caught numbers and a street.

A hard smile on his mouth, the Spider slid home the needle. Almost instantly, the man's lids dropped, his moans lightened.

A twig snapped behind Wentworth. He whirled, hand on gun. The white glare was full on him.

"Hoist them," a man's voice grated from the darkness. "Both hands high, Mr. Spider!"

CHAPTER 11
CITY OF DOOM

WENTWORTH CURLED his lips back from the fangs, his eyes burning through the slits of the black mask.

"Holy mother!" gasped the man in the shadows.

At his first syllable, Wentworth leaped, not toward the voice, but to a tree whose huge gnarled bole thrust into the edge of the headlight glare. The whip-crack of a long-barreled thirty-eight splashed crimson fire into the night. The lead burned across Wentworth's shoulders, made him stumble with the force of its sidewise slap. He spilled behind the protection of the tree, sprang up instantly.

The twin headlights of the motorcycle twisted about, but the hands that maneuvered them remained invisible in the blackness. Wentworth did not fire. That voice had held the accents of authority; that pistol had the ring of a police-positive revolver. The man behind the head lights probably was an officer, and Wentworth did not battle police with deadly lead.

Behind the tree, he dropped some stones into a pocket, then raised on tiptoes, feeling the bark. His fingers found a small knob and wrapped about it. He lifted himself with flexed arms, shot up a hand and found a limb. Still without using his feet, lest the leather rasp on the bark and betray his mode of flight, lest it scar the tree and leave a trail, he drew himself straight upward with bending arms, moved soundlessly among the thick growing limbs.

Below, the man moved the motorcycle, circling the tree. Now Wentworth could see him outlined against the brilliance, see the visored cap and putteed legs that confirmed his guess that the man was of the police. The man stopped the motorcycle and backed away into the night. Seconds later, his hand torch splashed light on the opposite side of the tree. A curse ripped from the man. He fanned the thickly growing shrubbery with his flashlight.

Wentworth tossed one of the stones he had picked up before climbing the tree, flipped it over beyond the edge of the torch's rays. Instantly the policeman whirled that way, his gun spewing lead and flame. He charged toward the sound, yelling, crashing through underbrush. Another stone thrown farther into the darkness lured him on. Wentworth dropped to the ground silently, jabbed his knife into the motorcycle's front tire, and stole away in the opposite direction. Finally he made his circuitous way to the road and found a police motorcycle parked there.

He spun it and, whipping the mask from his face, vaulted to the saddle as the engine roared into action. Within a hundred yards the speedometer needle passed eighty. The wind in Wentworth's nostrils choked him. He leaned far forward. On the long sweep down to Eatonville, the needle wavered past ninety. A touch of the siren scattered traffic, and minutes later Wentworth slowed to a squealing halt around the corner from the Bovita Street address the dying gangster had given him.

He cocked the light gray felt jauntily upon the brushy red hair of Patrick O'Roone and sauntered with a rolling swagger around into Bovita. Street. The house was frame and two stories tall and, very much the worse for paint, was squeezed in between a grocery and a shoe repair shop. Bovita for several blocks was spotted with such small stores, and a street car clanged and rattled along a single track down its middle.

Without a moment's hesitation, the swaggering figure that was Wentworth turned into the walk and moved deliberately up the steps. He knew the headquarters of such a gang would be well guarded, that an attempt to enter furtively would be much less likely to succeed than his frontal attack. For a moment before the door he paused, his practiced hand manipulating a lock pick. The bolt slid back silently, the knob and door moved without a sound. Wentworth walked boldly into the darkness, shut the door and stood listening.

FROM THE street came the retreating rattle of the street

NITA VAN SLOAN

car clattering over poorly laid rails, a swish of released air as it halted, then threshed on. The sound vibrated emptily in the house, vibrated and died. There came then, to Wentworth's ears, the faint rasp of claws on the floor.

Wentworth, cold chills of dread shuddering up his back, threw the minute beam of a small pocket flashlight ahead of him. He flinched back against the door, a cry in his throat. A giant cat was stalking him. It was snarling soundlessly, its' white-flecked lips baring needle teeth, its legs crouched for a spring. Its red eyes were wild with the maniacal rage of hydrophobia. And Wentworth dared not use his gun lest the police crash in.

That crouching beast, inching ever closer, with legs tensed to spring, told him the house was empty, that this headquarters had been deserted even as he forced its address from the moaning lips of that dying gangster. Wentworth's hand slid out a black-jack. He saw the cat cease its advance, its tail lashing slowly from side to side. He knew that when that tail stiffened, the cat would leap.

Wentworth sprang first. The cat reared on its hind legs, striking with spread claws. The blackjack flicked down, cracked upon the flat, broad head and smashed the cat, kicking to the floor.

Wentworth stepped clear of the threshing death and, guard-ing the gleam of the flash, swung it over the hall. He found closed doors to his right and bare, steep stairs leading upward on his left. Each of those dilapidated doors might conceal another such skulking killer as this cat, yet the place must be searched. In an abandoned office in Cologne, he had found a clue. Something here might point the way to the next step.

Deliberately Wentworth placed the flash between his teeth, stepped to the first door and flung it wide. Grasping the sill above it he jerked himself from the floor, swung his legs upward as a rush of tiny paws sounded below. Wentworth bent his head forward, and the beam of the light flashed on a dozen rushing gray backs, a charge of mad rats!

Waiting until the last had scampered past him, Wentworth swung forward and sprang into the middle of the room, slapping the door shut. His swift light found the room empty except for the death-stiffened figure of a dog. Not even a large dog. Not even a stick of furniture was in it. A closet was empty also.

In the next room, Wentworth's swift swung blackjack disposed of a hydrophobic cat, but his search was fruitless.

The second floor, when Wentworth had disposed of two more cats and a dog whose fangs drooled with death-laden foam, revealed a cheaply furnished office, another room where chairs grouped around a cigarette-scarred table that was littered with greasy cards and a third room which held only a mussed bed.

Wentworth frowned and began a more detailed search, wearing gloves of thin gray silk now to guard against leaving fingerprints. In a filthy bathroom he leaned close to inspect the mirror, drew out a magnifying glass and studied a black, greasy smear upon it. His face tightened with excitement. What he had found on the mirror was greasepaint, such as he himself used in his clever disguises!

Staring at the smear, Wentworth jerked his head about, listening. Stealthy footsteps creaked in the lower hall. The gangsters returning? Wentworth jerked his head in quick negative. The place had been definitely abandoned, or those death traps would not have been set. No, it must be the police. Of course, they had spotted that stolen motorcycle parked around the corner. Someone would have seen a swaggering red-head in a cocky gray hat enter the building....

Wentworth snatched up the body of the dog he had killed, holding it carefully by the leg. There was no danger of infection except from the animal's saliva. He eased up the window, peered out into a small yard behind the house. A man was crouched beside the door, a gun leveled. Wentworth smiled thinly.

He dropped the dog's body on the man's shoulders, felling him, and sprang down lightly as the policeman, yelling lustily with fear of the furry body, wrestled on the ground. As he struggled finally to his feet, Wentworth landed a single well timed right. He eased the policeman to the ground, placed the dog thoughtfully across his chest and loped out of the yard well ahead of the first men answering the policeman's cries.

A crowd was standing in the street, half of them peering toward the alley where the policeman had shouted, where Wentworth lurked.

Wentworth snatched off his hat, threw back his head and ran from the darkness as if desperate with fear.

"Mad dog!" he cried at the top of his lungs. "Mad dog!"

THE CROWD scattered like feathers before the wind. Wentworth was only one of a dozen running men and boys.

Within two blocks, he checked his mad dash to a brisk walk. No street car was in sight. No taxi. He headed directly across town for the flying field.

Though it was no more than eight o'clock, the street was virtually deserted. Many people had fled this pest hole, escaping from the scores of mad plague carriers loosed by the Master. Those scores had become hundreds now as rabid beasts infected others. Everywhere walked men with rifles, with pistols slung at their belts. They moved warily and kept a close eye on the shadows.

Wentworth paced beside one.

"Get any tonight?"

The man jerked a single glance at Wentworth.

"Two dogs," he said curtly, as his eye swung back to the darkness. "Two dogs and a cat."

"Mad?" asked Wentworth.

"Probably," the man replied. "Orders are to shoot all animals."

He walked on, and Wentworth kept pace with him past small identical cottages set on rectangular lawns as regularly spaced as squares on a checker board. Here and there were lights, but many houses were dark. As the two men neared a corner cottage, its door flung open and a woman plunged screaming from the porch. A boy of twelve ran behind her, dumb with fright.

A younger woman, apparently a maid, stumbled to the door behind them. Her head seemed heavy. She stepped out on the porch, and the sound of her heavy barking breath reached the two men on the walk fifteen feet away.

"That woman in the door has hydrophobia," Wentworth rasped out.

The mother heard and ran to him.

"Sylvie!" she panted. "Sylvie. My child, my baby!"

"What, ma'am?" asked the rifleman.

"My baby is in the house," the woman gasped out. "Upstairs. That girl...."

As the woman tugged at Wentworth's arm, a child of three in a nightgown toddled into the hallway behind the swaying girl.

The woman screamed. "Sylvie, go back!"

The child jumped out on the porch. "Mummie!" it cried in a shrill treble.

The voice caught the ear of the mad girl. She whirled, and Wentworth now saw the gleam of a knife in her hand. He started forward, as the child caught at her dress, raised her arms to the mad woman.

"Take baby," it said, and the childish treble carried through the night. The mother started to run forward as the knife swept up. Wentworth caught her aside, darted forward. But even as he ran, the guard's rifle spoke. The mad woman jerked to the impact of the bullet, reeled a half pace forward, knocking the baby down. The rifle spoke again and she pitched into the hallway and lay still.

The baby lay staring, a sob beginning in its throat. The mother stumbled up the steps, snatched her child, stood rocking it in her arms, her eyes fixed upon the body of the other woman. Wentworth, eyes hard, turned to the guard. The man's face was white and strained. He drew a hand across his forehead heavily so that it puckered the flesh.

"You don't feel as bad about it as I do," he muttered. "Hell!" The curse was explosive. "What can you do? The hospitals and the asylums are full of them. Every hour they bring in more, and they can't do nothing but let them die."

WENTWORTH LOOKED once at the woman cuddling her child, at the dead woman on the porch.

"Look out!" he cried, and his pistol spoke. Something threshed on the ground beside the porch, writhed out into the light—a mad dog.

Windows showed pale, staring faces. The guard slowly placed a charged cartridge in his rifle. Wentworth left him that way, strode up the street, his heels striking the pavement savagely. Within him, a high, white anger burned. It wiped him clean of the fatigue that had burdened his brain. No death man had ever devised could be harsh enough for the criminal who had loosed this hell upon earth!

A man walking with heavy slowness along the pavement ahead of him caught his eye. He led a boy by the hand, and he was mumbling to himself.

"I had to do it. "I had to kill her, son, You see." His words came to Wentworth, striding past. "Hey, mister," he asked, "where's the police station?"

Wentworth halted, stared at the man. "If you'll go down this street about four blocks, you'll find some police."

The man stared into Wentworth's face. His eyes were wide and without life, as the eyes of a man who had seen untenable horrors might be. "You see, mister," he said, "I had to kill her. She, she...."

Wentworth felt horror writhe like a cold snake within him. What was this man saying?"

"I had to kill her," the voice maundered on. "She went crazy, after the dog bit her. She was going to kill the boy, and...."

"Whom are you talking about?" Wentworth rasped.

"My wife," said the man, "I killed her."

Wentworth's teeth locked together. He whirled and strode away, with the man's mumbling in his ears. A man had killed his wife, driven mad by hydrophobia. A guard shot down a servant girl. The asylums were full, the hospitals jammed and helpless to do anything but wait for death. This rabies that struck with incredible speed, that spread death and crazy fear through this comfortable city of homes, still ran wild in the streets. Every lurking shadow might discharge a new menace, a dog with slashing fangs, a cat whose needle-like teeth....

Wentworth ground out a curse between his locked teeth. The new trail he followed had ended in a smear of grease paint. Now he must go back to Cologne and Washington Courthouse to seek a new lead to these monsters behind the plague.

Wentworth halted in mid-stride and leaped to the darkness beside an unlighted house as a screaming siren heralded a police car that side-slipped into the street with its engine roaring wide open. It rocketed past, whirled another corner.

Hurrying on, Wentworth heard the crashing of pistols, the racketing of a machine gun. Peering down the street where the police car had spun, he saw a blue-coated figure stretched on the sidewalk before a bank. Floodlights illuminated the scene like daylight. Men fired at the building from behind poles, from behind parked cars.

Wentworth's lips were drawn tight with bitter anger. These criminals were not content to stampede a city, to lay a third of its population writhing in the fatal madness of hydrophobia; they must loot and pillage in the wake of their slaughtering hordes. As Wentworth watched, the doors of the bank swung wide and a dozen furred beasts rushed out to the attack. Some police, panic-stricken, turned to flee. Others loosed their guns upon the harbingers of horrid death. Bullets from the bank mowed the men down.

CHAPTER 12
THE HORDES RUN WILD

F ROM HIS vantage point, Wentworth had a full view of the battle, the brightly lighted street, the black alley behind it. Yellow illumination flung suddenly into the shadows of that alley, showed a half dozen vague figures plunging to its cover. Wentworth raised his gun, braced against the side of the house which concealed him, then stayed his hand.

Above the crackling reports of the pistols, he caught the roar of an automobile engine and saw an unlighted car dart from the alley and race directly toward him. When it was a half block from the bank, its headlights flared out. Wentworth, a distorted smile on his mouth, deliberately sent an entire clip of bullets clawing through the auto. It staggered like a beast, spun to the left and hurled the curb. It smacked nose-on into a house and bounced back like a crumpled toy. Not a man ran from the wreck.

Grimly Wentworth reloaded, speeding on. Nothing back there for the Spider to do. The police were too close for him to affix his warning seal, and he need not worry about the gangsters' fate. If the police did not kill the survivors outright, they would third-degree from them any information they might possess and strike with the full force of that knowledge. No, the Spider need not delay.

93

As he hurried on across Eatonville, skirting horror on every side, he worked swiftly on his disguise. He had no time, and no need, to alter his appearance much. The gray hat went into a trash can, the wig to another. A cap came from his pocket. Then, a slouching walk to replace that bold-shouldered swagger of Patrick O'Roone and he was altered enough to baffle the police.

At the airport, he avoided Patrick O'Roone's chartered plane, hired another and sped back to Washington Courthouse where he sought some clue of Ram Singh. No one had seen him. The Hindu had vanished as completely as if the crocodiles of his native Ganges had trapped him in their maws. There was no help here.

He flew to Cologne, paid off the pilot and took a taxi to the city. It was nearly midnight. Once more he had been forced to abandon a disguise, and with it his hotel room and equipment. He went wearily to an all night restaurant to eat. A newspaper extra was scattered over a porcelain-topped table. Wentworth thrust aside the napkin holder and the mustard jar and spread the front page before him. As he read, his face set in a mold like steel and his eyes became diamond-hard. The hordes had struck again!

The people of two cotton mill towns in North Carolina had fled before the onslaught of the Mad Hordes of Doom... Banks and jewelry stores had been looted... An entire district of western wheat country had been evacuated after men in the fields had been attacked by rabid coyotes... Two ships, upon the Pacific had been battling for forty-eight hours an invasion of mad rats which had attacked and infected four sailors and as many passengers... The *Atlantica* speeding serum from L'Institut Pasteur reported that the entire shipment had been destroyed!

But these were minor tragedies beside the news that three steel towns scattered over Ohio and Indiana had received notice that if they were not evacuated within twenty-four hours, the dread hordes would be loosed upon them. As a foretaste, the Horde Master had let six mad wolves run berserk through the streets, infecting scores before they were shot down. And on the forehead of each animal had been the burned brand of the Master's death-head brand!

People were evacuating two of the towns at once, the paper reported. The third was preparing a defense, close mesh fences, machine guns, marksmen with stacks of ammunition. In advance they were wiping out the town's population of rats with hydro-cyanic gas, dogs and cats were being executed by the hundreds. **WENTWORTH AROSE** from the table. In a washroom he removed the last vestiges of disguise, became in fact Richard Wentworth, who carried the credentials and gold badge of the Federal Department of Justice.

In that identity, he took rooms at the Cologne-Vanderbilt and put through a series of calls. He ordered Jackson, the ex-sergeant of the A.E.F who served as his chauffeur, to fly to Cologne with his slot-winged scarlet Northrup and its equipage of sub-machine guns. He phoned Washington and got autho-rization to act in Ohio on the hydrophobia murders as endan-gering the public health of the nation; he found that Professor

Brownlee already was on the way West—that Nita had left hours before and should already have reached the Healy home.

It was too soon to go to the Healy home. He could enter the Castle easily as a federal investigator, but felt it would be better to seem simply a friend of Nita Van Sloan. Fatigue pressed upon him. Sitting bolt upright in a chair, assembling the jigsaw bits of the problem that had proved so far unsolvable, Wentworth felt an immense weariness, a sense of hopelessness such as had not oppressed him before in all the years of his ceaseless battling against the Underworld. He had struck a few painful blows, but he was as far this day from learning the headquarters of the gang and locating its leader as he had been when first that news item about the A.S.P.C.A. protest had caught his attention.

Wentworth retraced, step by step, his battle against the gang, the maniac attack which had led him to Healy's home, the death of the guard when Scarlet offered him a drink, the mad cats that attacked him, the loss of Ram Singh, the pursuit of the truck and the loosing of the first of the hordes on Eatonville. In all that chase, only two things presented themselves as tangible clues. The Dr. Brent against whom Rusk had gasped a dying warning was actually involved in the case, and the gang's headquarters in Eatonville had revealed a smear of grease paint on a mirror.

Of all the baffling facts of this many sided case, that was the most puzzling. Somehow, Wentworth felt, that grease paint held the key to the entire affair of the Mad Hordes of Doom.

He arose wearily, checked his automatic and, placing it ready to his hand, threw himself down on the bed for the first sleep he had had in sixty hours of ceaseless struggle and death.

Less than an hour later, the continuous ringing of the telephone aroused him. He sprang instantly to his feet, automatic in hand, stared blankly at the phone. The heaviness of fatigue still clouded his brain. He jerked his head sharply, crossed to the instrument.

"Richard Wentworth speaking," he said quietly. The voice on the wire was that of his fiancée, Nita Van Sloan. "Dick," she said, "something horrible is threatening this house. I'm not quite sure yet where it will strike, but it's here and the blow may fall at any minute. No one is planning to sleep tonight."

"Definite information, darling," Wentworth asked her, "or just suspicions?"

Nita hesitated. "I have information, but nothing definite," she said finally. "Could you come at once? I told them I was going to call on a friend here who was an excellent shot."

"In half an hour," Wentworth promised.

IT WAS twenty-five minutes to the dot from the time he hung up till his taxi snubbed to a halt at the iron-barred gates of the Castle. At Wentworth's name, two guards opened the way and the taxi muttered up the winding road with its watching black trees, to the gray bulk of the Castle itself, ghostly in the white light of the moon. Despite the balmy warmth of the night, every window was tightly closed. Wentworth climbed broad stone steps to doors of studded iron that arched high above him. At his touch a dangling rope sounded a solemn bell note within. A butler opened the door, but Nita herself was there to greet him, her white hands outstretched to his, her red lips smiling a welcome that was shadowed by a fear which haunted her blue eyes. She was grace itself in a clinging gown of black.

She gave the faintest shake of her chestnut curls, clustering close about an aristocratically poised head, and Wentworth, his face still formal, only bent above her hands.

"Nice of you to come so soon, Richard," Nita said, "I think I'll have need of your championship shooting before long.

Wentworth raised his smooth black brows, brows that arched to quirky points in which there lurked always a hint of raillery. "My good right eye is ever at thy service." His smile was gay.

Nita led him into the high ceilinged drawing room with its gaunt, draped walls of stone. The fireplace yawned like a black mouth. The occupants of the room were the same as on that other night when Wentworth had crashed through the French doors to warn them that a maniac was creeping on the house. They seemed more fearful now than they had at that first dread warning.

The two men and women were in a close group beneath a lamp that threw brittle white light upon the powdered shoulders of the women, upon the formal black and white of the men. Healy, his wife and daughter and Scarlet sat at cards, about a low, square table."

At Wentworth's entrance, Healy threw his cards in a slithering heap upon the leather top. "You saved me from a terrific beating, Mr. Wentworth," he said, with an attempt at rough jocularity which fell strangely flat. "Four hearts, redoubled.

Four hearts, redoubled. Wentworth glanced under amused brows at the four, at Healy and the dark, tragic warmth of Sybil Healy, to the glowing golden blonde of her daughter, Doris. Scarlet was standing, his shoulders so stooped that he seemed to lean, his small mouth puckered into a welcoming smile. Shadows were black all about them. In the doorway of the music room behind them, a butler stood like a sentinel.

"Which one of them do you want me to shoot, Nita?" Wentworth asked, smiling.

Scarlet's eyes jerked wide an instant, then the puckery smile widened. "Ah, I see. It's just a pleasantry."

Healy shook his head with its close cap of steel gray hair. "It wouldn't be much of a surprise if somebody did walk in and offer to shoot one of us," he said, heavily. There was an expression of keen interest on Wentworth's intensely vital face as Nita made introductions. Such was the force of his personality that his mere entrance into the room seemed to have relieved the tension. Doris Healy sat less rigidly in her chair, and Healy's square, unsmiling face seemed less drawn.

"I see I've been missing some fun," said Wentworth. "Will I really get a chance to do some shooting?"

A small door, half hidden in the shadow by the hearth, flung open and Doris jerked erect with a small cry choked in her throat. Sybil's hand flew to Scarlet's arm, then both women relaxed as the same curly-headed youth Wentworth had seen there before came striding into the room.

"Who is this man?" he demanded, pointing a dramatic arm at Wentworth.

Healy snorted breath out hard through his nose. Contempt was plain on his face. He deliberately turned square-set shoulders on the youth.

Nita walked before Wentworth, "Richard," she said, "this is Jack Collins, who has been very kind. Jack, this is Richard Wentworth, a friend of mine."

Wentworth bowed. Collins tossed a dangling lock of hair from his forehead, took two strides forward and clasped Wentworth's hand in a solid, brown grip.

"I'm glad to meet you, suh."

He said it seriously and looked as if he meant it. He turned then and crossed to Doris' chair, bent over her shoulder.

"Mighty sorry I startled you, Go'geous," he said. "The guards told me a strange man had come in and I thought I'd bettuh investigate."

The girl's smile up at him was completely forgiving. Her glance swept coldly past Nita.

"If you'll come into the library," said Healy, abruptly to Wentworth, "I'll tell you just what's been going on here. I'd like to have a sane man's view on it. Looks to me like we're all a little cracked here." He bowed to Nita jerkily. "If you'll pardon the liberty of my including you. You've been here long enough to get the poison into your mind, too."

IN THE library, Wentworth saw that the high single window had a new pane. Healy went over in detail the happenings of the hours since Wentworth, in his disguise as Sven Gustafsson, had cried a warning into the quiet house. There had been a series of attacks, especially at nights. Mad dogs had fairly rained on the place. A guard had been bitten, yet there had been no attempt to enter the Castle itself.

"Didn't this guard who died at your place," Wentworth asked, "mention some doctor named Brent?"

Healy nodded. "But police found no trace of him."

"Ever know a man named Brent who would have any reason to hate you?"

Healy stared fixedly at Wentworth.

"You're just a friend of Miss Van Sloan who can shoot straight?" There was a slight jeer in his voice.

"That was for your family and guests," said Wentworth. He laid a small gold badge on the arm of Healy's chair. The capitalist's eyes narrowed on it, raised swiftly to the vital strength of Wentworth's face.

"I see," he said slowly. "No... never knew a man named Brent."

Wentworth arose. "I don't think you need worry any more in the immediate future about attacks by animals," he said.

"Have you noticed, Mr. Healy, that though there have been a number of personal attacks on you, there has not been a single blow struck at one of your industrial towns, steel, or cotton, or wheat, or your ships—although against rival lines there have been repeated attacks?"

Healy stared fixedly up into Wentworth's eyes and rose slowly to face him.

"I'll ask you to explain that statement," he said heavily. There was menace in his bearing.

Wentworth shrugged. His face was a smiling mask that told Healy nothing.

"I just pointed out an obvious fact," he said. "I see nothing to explain. I might add, however, that the attacks upon you have so far proved abortive."

Healy continued to stare into Wentworth's eyes. Am I to consider myself under arrest?" he asked quietly.

Wentworth raised his brows. Their mockery was increased.

"Such a question, Mr. Healy! Shall we join the ladies?"

Their eyes locked. Healy hesitated, but presently moved toward the door. "I would rather," said Wentworth, "that you would not mention my identity. Be careful that no mad dogs bite you, Mr. Healy."

He strolled off toward where Nita stood idly turning the pages of a magazine. She raised her head of clustering curls and her eyes were questioning. Wentworth smiled, fingered the pages of the magazine as if he were interested in it.

"Darling, could you, without too much chicanery, make the charming Mr. Collins appear deeply er—interested?"

Nita followed his lead, pointing to an advertisement and looking up at him with a laugh. "And if I can?"

"I will see if I cannot similarly beguile Mrs. Healy."

Nita straightened with a thoughtful air. "I don't see the maneuver very clearly. Of course, it places Doris and Scarlet together...."

Wentworth smiled, turned to the others. "I have an entertainment to suggest," he said, raising his voice, "that I think will prove more exciting than bridge."

They all turned toward him, Sybil Healy twisting lithely in

her chair, Doris turning a mildly puzzled glance. Young Collins frowned above his cards.

"Let's all take a walk," said Wentworth, "in the garden."

A rough exclamation jerked out of Healy. "But I've just told you that mad dogs and cats prowl the grounds. One man is dead. Another has been bitten…."

Wentworth smiled at him. "I'm an excellent shot," he said, touching the lapel of his coat. He turned toward Sybil Healy. "And, may I have the honor?" he asked.

CHAPTER 13
DEATH WAITS IN THE GARDEN

FOR AN instant the woman stared at Wentworth with eyes that widened slowly. Plainly she thought him mad. But as she met the challenge of his gaze, her face softened and she got slowly to her feet. She tossed her head.

"Why not?" she demanded.

"A walk in the garden!" Scarlet exclaimed. "That's an excellent idea!" There was eagerness in his voice.

Wentworth smiled at the thin, stoop shouldered man as he rose quickly. Despite his slightly unhealthy appearance, there was a certain attractiveness about him, an aspect of bored experience that would be irresistible to many women, to discontented wives, perhaps, or to very young girls.

"And you?" Wentworth turned to the scowling Collins.

"I think it's utter nonsense," Collins said vehemently. He got to his feet, taller than Wentworth by an inch and thick with the brawn that college football builds.

"Ooh," said Nita at Wentworth's side. "I choose him!"

"She thrust out a finger in childish mimicry at Collins.

He stared at her in bewilderment.

"Why," cried Nita, artlessly, "aren't you going walking?"

He was too young to be proof against that, too young to turn angrily away as Healy was doing.

"If you're demented enough to go," snapped Healy, "you're going under full guard."

He jangled a loud bell violently, and a man popped in at the door. "Order four men with rifles to stand watch over these fools. They're going walking!"

"Really, my dear Healy," protested Scarlet, "you're taking all the fun out of the thing, you know."

Healy roared at him. "Have you gone mad, too? Remember it's my wife and daughter!"

"Both ably protected," Wentworth assured him.

He saw Nita laugh up at Collins, saw that young man reluctantly relax his scowl and grin back, saw them saunter toward the French doors that opened on a stone terrace and formal garden beyond. He offered his arm to Sybil Healy. She opened her slightly pouting lips, and her white teeth showed. The shimmering saffron of her gown revealed the quickened rise and fall of her breasts. She put her hand on Wentworth's arm. Scarlet offered his to Doris, and the six of them moved toward the double, glass-paned doors.

Nita lagged a little as she neared them, but Collins strode

swing-shouldered forward and thrust the doors wide. The balmy softness of the night drifted in filled with the rasped chorus of insects. The moon was silver. Nita and Collins walked on, Nita with both hands on his arm, looking up intently into his face. Wentworth smiled secretly and turned to find his partner watching as Scarlet and her daughter moved off along a shrubbery-bordered path. Doris seemed nervous. She walked very close to Scarlet.

"Do you have any preference of direction?" Wentworth murmured, and Sybil Healy started, turned her head a shade too quickly away from the sauntering pair.

"Oh, no," she said, then waved her hand vaguely in the direction Scarlet and Doris had taken. Wentworth assented, but they did not move along the same path. He chose one parallel to it.

They had not taken fifty slow paces when a scream of torture rang out, punctuated by three swift shots!

WENTWORTH HURDLED a low hedge, sprinted along a winding path and spun around a high clump of bushes to find Doris tight in Scarlet's arms. From his right hand dangled a pistol, and Wentworth stared beyond them where a huddled form was stretched on the earth. The ray of his flashlight revealed a dead wolf whose rear paw had been chained to a small tree. Upon the wolfs forehead was burned the death's head of the Horde Master!

"You had all the luck," Wentworth said regretfully. "And you do shoot well. All three bullets dead center."

"Doris!" The rasp of Sybil Healy's voice startled Wentworth.

He turned toward her. "Doris," she repeated. "Go to your room at once. You must rest. That beast must have given you a frightful scare. "No—" Scarlet had started to help Doris toward the house… "I'll attend to her."

Collins panted up with Nita. He strode toward Doris, and her mother released her to him.

"What happened, Go'geous?" the boy asked solicitously.

Scarlet and Wentworth smiled at each other. Sybil Healy thrust between them.

"And as for you," she addressed Wentworth in a voice whose harshness belied the soft lines of her face. "You should have had more sense than to suggest any such fool adventure as this."

"Yes, Mrs. Healy," said Wentworth meekly. "Perhaps we'd better go in now."

He offered his arm to Nita and they moved off toward the house. A butler met them on the terrace. "A phone call, sir, long distance for Mr. Wentworth."

Wentworth strode into the house. Healy glowered at him. "You may take the call in my library."

Wentworth nodded his thanks, walked into the book-lined room and casually closed the door behind him. He listened for moments with narrowed eyes, his face whitening.

"The time has come for desperate measures," he said. "Slow progress will no longer help. I'll go to Hurzon tonight. General Lansing, eh? Will you see that he knows I'm coming there and recognizes my power? Yes, I want it known publicly, too."

He laughed shortly. "You can do what you damned please. I'm playing a lone hand and I'm doing it my way. Very well then, I'll tender my resignation." He smiled with lips thinned as he said it. "I thought you'd see it my way," he said firmly, and looked up to find Nita standing inside the door.

"Washington," he said, as he hung up. "I think I'll send in my resignation anyway. The credentials help on occasion, but they can't seem to learn. I'll work in my own way, or not at all."

"What are your desperate measures, Dick?" she asked, quietly. "Can't I help?"

Wentworth crossed to her, folded her in his arms. "Darling, you can help me most by staying right here. Watch Healy."

"Watch *Healy!*"

Wentworth nodded. "I just received word that at Ashokan where they tried to fight off the hordes, mad bats*—they must be vampires obtained in some way from South America—flew over the fences and attacked men. The town was evacuated after that. The gangsters got more than half a million from the banks."

"Is that what's behind all this, Dick?"

Wentworth shook his head. "No dear. That's only, part of it, The plot is industrial; and if it isn't checked soon, it's going to paralyze half the factories in the country. All rivals of a certain man are being wiped out so that his plants will become the greatest in the world, so that he will operate a virtual monopoly.

---

* AUTHOR'S NOTE: Carini of I'lnstitut Pasteur reported of a plague that destroyed about four thousand cattle and one thousand horses in Sao Paulo, Brazil, that he was convinced rabic vampire bats were responsible, viz. Ann. de I'lnst. Pasteur, Paris, Nov. XXV, 11, p785.

"Meanwhile, during the build-up, his plants aren't up to the demands. Work is being shut down all over the country for lack of the materials these plants should produce. It's creating another national crisis. And all so that one man can benefit!"

"That man is Healy?" Nita's breath was quick. At Wentworth's assent, she began, "Then why not...."

"Why not arrest him?" Wentworth finished. "That would do no good at all, dear. You just leave that to me."

He swiftly made his excuses to the household—an unexpected business call would necessitate his departure—and borrowed a car in which he made a headlong race for Cologne. He made rapid arrangements there, found by phone that Professor Brownlee had set up a work shop and under heavy guard was busy on some means of combating the Mad Hordes. Then Wentworth went to the airport, got out his scarlet Northrup and set it racing into the northwest.

Hurzon, second largest of the nation's steel towns, had been warned that all its workers must flee or the Mad Hordes would wipe them out. If the Horde Master won in this assault, there would be no stopping him!

CHAPTER 14
"DESPERATE MEASURES"

HURZON SPRAWLED out on the prairies of Indiana like a vast black octopus, an army of huts about each plant that erupted from the soil.

Wentworth slanted through the smoky atmosphere, set down

his speedy Northrup on the crossed, concrete runways of the landing field and taxied up to the hangars labeled *GUESTS* with large black letters.

There was a squadron of army planes on the line, and as Wentworth climbed out on the wing two soldiers marched up with bayoneted rifles.

The men's challenge was sharp, but at Wentworth's query for headquarters, they became more respectful and passed him through a series of lines to the offices of Brigadier-General Francis Lansing.

The general sat behind a varnished yellow desk like a man at bay, grasping its edge with thin, nervous hands. At Wentworth's name he jerked to his feet, and strode, spare and tall, to seize his hand.

"I don't generally welcome civilian advice." He snapped out his words like shots. "Not generally, but I'll be glad to co-operate with you, Wentworth. Anyone the President recommends...."

"Before we start," Wentworth told General Lansing, "there are certain arrangements I'd like to make. Will you have your oldest and weakest armored car segregated for my exclusive personal use? I'll drive it myself."

General Lansing studied him with calculating bright eyes and jabbed a punch bell on his desk violently. An orderly popped in, stiff as a rifle, received orders to call a car—the general gave its number.

"Don't worry about that," Wentworth told the general, "but if you can spare a man to follow me and report to you where I go, we may be able to trap the Master of the Hordes. Now then, this is what I have learned about the methods of these criminals…."

When the conference was over, Wentworth went directly to the car, an awkward closed machine with straight sides of gray-painted steel and a narrow slit for vision which was covered with bulletproof glass. It was a model of 1929, Wentworth recognized, and nodded with satisfaction. There was a powerful motor beneath that slab-sided hood. He climbed in, kicked the starter and began a bumping, slow patrol of the lines.

Frequently he alighted and walked along the barricades that were being thrown about the town. A close-mesh inner fence had been completed and twenty paces from it another, supported by entanglements of wire with inch long barbs, was being erected. A few scattered houses outside had been deserted.

WENTWORTH CLIMBED back into the car and trundled on. He moved alertly, though he had had less than an hour's rest in seventy-two, hours of unending battle, seventy-two hours in which the nation had tasted of terror and death, of madness and wild panic. There were harsh lines about his compressed lips. His eyes were sunken but burned with a restless fire, and pounds seemed to have dropped from his body that was as lean as rawhide. Yet his fierce will, his sharp intelligence seemed to need no rest.

"You'll wear yourself out before the battle starts," General Lansing rumbled, studying him speculatively with his small bright eyes while Wentworth snatched dinner with him.

"My job's almost done," Wentworth said cheerfully. "They'll probably attack around midnight."

"I'd guess dawn," Lansing said.

Wentworth nodded. "Perfect, if you want troops worn out with waiting, but the Master of the Hordes wants men tense and nervous, so that panic will threaten."

At ten, Wentworth resumed his plodding patrol, bumping over lanes that had grown familiar now. At eleven-thirty, he alighted beside a machine gun embrasure and walked toward the men. One sat upon the tripod of a gun, his head sagging on his chest. He got sluggishly to his feet, breathing hard.

With a cold fear racing down his back, Wentworth heard the man's breath become hoarse in his throat so that he sighed noisily with each exhalation. He snatched out a flash light and threw its beam into the man's eyes.

The soldier started back, leaned heavily against the gun shield, and Wentworth saw his throat muscles work. For an instant he sagged there inertly, then his face convulsed and he sprang for Wentworth; snatching for the bayonet at his side. His breath was like the barking of a dog. Wentworth knew those dread symptoms of hydrophobia. His fist flashed and he knocked the man flat. The three other soldiers sprang forward. "Attention!" Wentworth snapped. His voice crackled with authority. The men halted uncertainly and when the command was repeated they stiffened.

"That man knocked down is sick," Wentworth said curtly. Bind his arms and take him to the hospital, you and you." He designated two of the men, saw them start their task and,

springing to his car, sent it leaping over the rats to headquarters. He slapped open the door, burst into the general's office where three officers were bowed over a map.

"I found a soldier suffering from hydrophobia," Wentworth bit out. "I think he's only one of many."

General Lansing jerked to his feet. "Every one of the men was examined carefully," he said. "It's ridiculous—"

The breach was unguarded except
for Wentworth's single gun.

"I found one," Wentworth pointed out. "The rest is sheer guesswork, but it would be superb strategy on the part of our enemy to infect enough of the soldiers to demoralize the force.

Remember, the Master of the Hordes has this virus developed to the point that it strikes within thirty-six hours. He may be able to time it just when he is ready to attack."

The other three officers were openly skeptical. General Lansing frowned, standing rigidly behind his desk, his jaw muscles knotting. The phone jangled and Lansing snatched it up.

"Yes," he said crisply. "Very well, take him to the hospital. Notify the sergeants that they are to shoot at once any man so stricken during action!"

He slapped up the receiver. "Another case," he said rapidly, caught up the phone again. "Colonel Roberts… Colonel, two cases of hydrophobia have been found among the men. Make an immediate inspection of all the troops and segregate any of which you are at all suspicious."

WENTWORTH WAITED for no more. He sped to his car, shot it back to the lines. Already doctors, each with an armed attendant, were hastening toward the troops.

It was ten minutes of twelve when Wentworth, jerked to a halt again at the line. He stepped down. A shot cracked in the darkness twenty yards beyond the barbed wire where pickets stood watch. As if that had been a signal, another, softer sound made itself heard, a splashing of water. Wentworth whirled, flung the ray of a pocket flashlight toward the dilapidated huts behind him. The beam glinted on a hose nozzle, on a silvery stream of water that strengthened even as he watched it until it broke in a spray of glistening drops against the fence.

Choking back a shout, Wentworth darted to the hose and

screwed the nozzle shut. He smashed against the door of the hull and plunged in, slashing the darkness with his light as with his word. The house was empty. Whoever had loosed the water had fled. Wentworth darted back outside. Still the soft splashing of water sounded and above it came other sounds, horrible with their senselessness, the screams of madmen!

TWO SHOTS cut the night twenty feet away, and two men pitched screaming to the ground. An officer crouched over them with a smoking pistol. His sharp voice grew harsh in command. The crack of revolvers came from every side. Wentworth flung to his car, switched on its headlights. As far as their blue-white brilliance penetrated through the night, he saw glistening streams of water at intervals of fifty feet. Soldiers were choking them off, but their hellish errand had been fulfilled. Well Wentworth knew that the Master of the Hordes had bribed workmen within the fences to loose those streams of water—planning that the sight and sound of it should hurl into homicidal rages the soldiers he had injected with the virus of the mad death.

The scream of the stricken men, the crack of pistols still echoed over the brittlely tense battle line when Wentworth heard two ripping explosions, saw bunched spears of flame stab upward from the fences fifty yards to his right. Torn bodies were in that flame, and the screams of the wounded mingled with the cries of the madmen.

Like an echo of that first double blast, another and another tore out to left, to right, to the rear. All along the lines, the enemy had blasted the fences, making way for the Mad Hordes!

A reserve squad went past on the double to reinforce the

dynamited troops. Two men were lagging. The sergeant spat an order at them. Without warning, one of the soldiers jerked up his rifle and shot down the officer. He whirled savagely on his companion, slashed at him with his bayonet. His face, illuminated by the white glare of a floating Very light, was twisted insanely. Wentworth shot him through the head. The second soldier whirled, throwing up his rifle, and Wentworth sped a second bullet.

The reserve jogged off to its task, but the men moved reluctantly with backward flung glances at the bodies on the ground. Would they stand firm when the Mad Hordes poured through the breaches?

Rifles popped like a string of firecrackers. The ground beyond the fences, white as day beneath luminance of floodlights, was strewn with the carcasses of slain dogs, but others and still others poured from the darkness.

They moved, with the stiff mechanical jerkiness of automatons, unswerving.

Drooling jaws agape, they loped toward the breaches in the fence, springing over the bodies of the dead. Soundless they were in attack or wounded. Struck once, they dragged onward until they were shot again or until they managed to penetrate the line. They snapped at each other, gashing the flanks of dogs that ran beside them, receiving bloody tears in their own hides. But they stopped for nothing.

They did not fight among themselves or with men. A snap of their jaws and they were gone into the blackness of the night.

Wentworth threw his car across the breach and loosed a

sub-machine gun in bursts upon those that got past the enfi-lading fire of the soldiers. Even above the crackling of guns, he could hear the fearful cries of men, struck from the rear by their own companions gone mad, or pulled down by the Hordes. He saw a great slinking cat leap upon a man's back and the two tumbled in a tangled mass that made it impossible to shoot. It might have been a war of the Beasts against Mankind.

FOR A few seconds, the waves of mad dogs ceased, then terribly from the night swept the most horrible of all those mad hundreds that had charged upon the beleaguered city-mad wolves whose foreheads bore the grinning brand of the Master of the Hordes, the death head! A dozen unnerved soldiers within Wentworth's range of vision whirled to flee, but were driven back by the flaming revolvers of their officers.

On rushed the wolves, slashing through the bright lights in a half dozen lightning bounds. They left some of their fellows dead upon the ground, but most of them charged even through Wentworth's deadly fire. The soldiers broke from all control, broke and ran backward, sweeping their officers with them. Upon their flanks ran the terribly silent wolves with their fearful brand of death. Their long white madness-laden fangs gashed into the men.

And, horror on top of horror, Wentworth saw a black-winged form flit through the light. An officer who had been knocked down by his retreating men reeled to his feet, stumbled to a machine-gun to continue the vain battle. The black thing wheeled toward him and the man's face vanished in an embrace of leathern wings. The man's scream was high and cracked with fear. He tore the thing from his face, hurled it savagely to the ground and ground his heels upon it.

From the darkness, two more of the black forms wheeled, struck at his white and fear-ridden face, the officer whipped at them with flailing arms, turned and ran desperately.

The Master of the Hordes had released the bats, his plague of mad vampires!

What could guns and fences avail against these? The breach was unguarded by the dead and Wentworth's single gun. Cats still slunk among the dead and slipped through the opening or clawed over the fences. Scampering gray crawling things that were rats and mice poured past. Guns were useless against that horde. In the hovels of the town they would find ample concealment, and thousands of their fellows to spread the infection they brought.

Wentworth ceased his futile firing. Silence shut down about him, silence broken only by the groans of the wounded, the distant thin popping of guns where the defense still held for the moment—these, and the scampering, stealthy, murderous feet of the Hordes.

HIS MOUTH a grim, hard line, Wentworth started the car and turned it toward the breach. The battle had been fought and lost. It was time for his "desperate measures."

Wentworth pushed on, nosing along a street that was black as death. On the far eastern horizon, the moon crept into view like a lop-sided, blood-shot eye. Somewhere back here, Wentworth knew, were the leaders of this fearful attack, somewhere here the brain that had engineered this utter route of soldiers and machine guns, who had accomplished the doom of another town. Banks were being pillaged back in the city, jewelry stores looted of their wealth, the homes of the rich ransacked. The town was doomed.

Without warning, there was a smashing explosion behind Wentworth. He jerked his head about to find that a pit had been blasted in the road. Even as he stared the armored car jarred and trembled to a second ripping upheaval. He jammed on brakes, slid to a halt on the verge of another bomb-hole.

"Surrender," a voice called, "or the next bomb will be under the car. Be sensible, Wentworth."

Wentworth switched out his headlights, loosed his machine gun at the voice. He spun the steering wheel, jolted over a ditch and charged toward the sound. More bombs exploded around him.

A grim smile twitched Wentworth's mouth. He had half a drum of ammunition left for his machine gun, three clips of cartridges for his automatic. He loosed the half drum in a ripping roll of fire that rattled through the walls of the house before him. He wanted to be captured. He had made himself conspicuous, in this armored car all day, he had pushed out beyond the last defenses for that sole purpose, but he didn't intend to yield too easily.

The machine gun emptied its last ripping blast and Wentworth dropped the overheated weapon. With his pistol he waited, and waiting, he felt a drowsiness stealing over him. He kicked open ventilators but the sleepiness increased.

He moved loggily toward the door and machine gun bullets

racketed against its heavy steel. Wentworth knew he was being gassed. With his last gleam of consciousness, he raised his automatic and poured a stream of hot lead through the ignition switch, then he relaxed.

The Spider had employed his "desperate measures." If you can't find the enemy, let the enemy find you!

CHAPTER 15
HUMAN GUINEA PIGS

THE BLACKNESS lifted slowly and became a cloudy gray. Semi-conscious, Wentworth was acutely aware of sensory stimuli. Points dug into the flesh of his back and legs, yet he was powerless to move. All about him he seemed to hear the slow-timed barking of dogs. A man was screaming hoarsely, without words, over and over again one high-pitched, cracked scream. A stench like the closed monkey house of a zoo was heavy.

Those points in his back were uncomfortable. Wentworth sought to move and relieve the stabbing pressure. His legs twitched and he heard a dry chuckle.

"I thought it was about time you came around, Mr. Wentworth," a voice as rasping as a rusty hinge creaked out. "I'll retire until you're able to chat."

Wentworth gathered his sleeping will to force himself back to consciousness. He moved a hand heavily and dropped it beside him. He felt a wooden floor and straw. Straw... was that what stabbed his back? His hand touched his side and felt bare flesh.

Wentworth's eyes began to focus clearly and he saw black vertical bars. The barking sounds were clearer, the high, terrible screaming went on. He braced his hands, forced himself to a sitting position, and realized two things; he was stark naked and was seated upon the floor of a cell enclosed by close-set iron bars!

"I would have awakened you sooner, but you looked as if you needed sleep. And strong, rested men make the best virus," the voice said.

Wentworth echoed the words in his mind. Was this man, his captor, planning to make him work to produce hydrophobia germs? He shook his head heavily, braced hands and legs and reeled to his feet, stood staring as he swayed in the dazzling light. It was switched off abruptly and the monotonous scream-ing resumed.

"Can't you stop that noise," he demanded in irritation.

The dry chuckle came to him again and now his eyes made out a small, stooped figure outside the cell, a bent little old man with stringy white hair that straggled thinly about a peaked head.

"In just a little while," the man promised. You aren't half as impatient to stop that noise as the fellow that's making it. But it isn't time yet."

Behind the stooped figure of the little man he made out the bars of other cages. Men stood in all of them, mother naked, gripping the bars and staring. And with the suddenness of a stabbing pain Wentworth realized what that barking sound was. It was the breathing of these men! And men who breathed like that—Good Lord! *These men all had hydrophobia!*

SLOWLY, HE turned his head to right and left. More cages. Fully thirty men imprisoned at the whim of this dry voiced torturer. The screams… Wentworth stared into the cage next to his own. The man was a giant Negro standing six feet three in his bare feet. His head was thrown back. His breath was a groan and with each panted exhalation he cried terribly. His knees were sagging, but he held himself erect with great fists gripping the bars.

"Perhaps you… are thirsty," came the dry voice of the stooped man, timing his words to fall between the screams "The gas… affects you… that way."

"In heaven's name, no!" cried Wentworth, but only the dry laughter answered him and the man poured water from a gurgling bottle into a glass.

"Better drink… while you can," he said, and handed the glass to Wentworth.

A hell of screaming broke loose in the room. Men fell down and writhed on the floor, gripping their tormented throats. The giant rolled his great head from side to side in agony. His knees sagged more and more until he was holding himself erect by his hands alone. A man diagonally across from Wentworth shouted a scream of filthy curses. He demanded death for himself in a cry that could he heard even above the bedlam of pain and madness. He begged for it, though it was plain the madness did not grip him yet.

Wentworth turned from the torture and walked to the back of his cell. There in darkness he drank the glass of water. He was thirsty, yet he did not wish to torture those other poor unfortunates dying of hydrophobia. In the name of heaven, what could be the purpose of all this torture?

"Why not shoot that poor Negro? he asked. "His death is a matter of hours and there is no need for him to suffer."

The ugly, peaked head of the bent man shook from side to side. He hobbled from the room, being careful to keep clear of the hands outthrust to grab him between bars. He went out a small door at one end of the hall of the cages.

When he returned, the bedlam had died. He had with him two men who were thrusting ahead of them a third man.

The two men were clothed. The third was naked, his head was clipped and the corded muscles stood out like ropes on his brown body as he fought his captors. They thrust him up to the cage in which Wentworth stood, then held a gun on Wentworth while they unlocked the door and thrust him in.

"Greetings to thee, Ram Singh," Wentworth greeted the newcomer quietly. "I had thought thee dead."

"On thee the salaam," said the captive, bowing and touching a cupped hand to his forehead. He answered as Wentworth had spoken, in Hindustani. "Soon, *sahib*, we *will* be dead." On his upper right arm was a festering wound, a wound as if from human teeth!

Ram Singh bowed and touched his forehead. "It is a shame upon me, *sahib*, that I allowed this offal of a dog to capture me. *Wah!* If I but had my knife!"

123

"They tricked you, oh, Ram Singh?"

From without, the mad little man shouted abuse. They ignored him. The Hindu grinned like a wolf, lips thin against his fine white teeth, "Two of the dogs tasted my steel, *sahib*, before some vile vapor made my muscles like a woman's and three of them

The girl was thrust before the cage. Wentworth grasped
the bars and fury sent his brain spinning.

fell upon me. *Wah!* They were cowards! Five of them to seize
me!" His voice grew harsh.

"May Allah deliver them to my knife!"

Wentworth shook his head slowly. "There is no disgrace when thy enemies bare thy head, Oh, Ram Singh."

He told his faithful servant then how he had allowed himself to be captured so that he might learn where the headquarters of the gang were situated. The impatient snarling of the bent old man who was their captor broke in on them.

"May you have the joy of your reunion," the man rasped. "Shall I worry when my guinea pigs turn their backs upon me?"

His guinea pigs! Wentworth faced slowly about, walked to the bars. In heaven's name, what could the fiend mean?

"Listen, old fool," he said curtly. "We must remain here for a little while, of course, but it behooves you to be civil while we are here."

The man giggled. He spat at Wentworth's face. "You think the soldier you had following you can give the alarm? I've got him in the other room. No, my dear Wentworth, you are beyond help!"

Wentworth, smiled calmly into his sneering face. It stirred the man's anger. "I know! I know!" he screamed. "You are the man they call the Spider. When we captured your body servant, we traced him and found that out. But this once the Spider won't win. The Spider never before met Dern Bierkson." He tapped his hollow chest with a claw-like hand. "Shall I tell you what will happen to this mighty man who calls himself the Spider? Did you wonder at the swiftness with which the germs of hydrophobia struck? I did that, I"—once more he tapped his thin chest—"Even as old Pasteur built up his fixed virus by giving the disease to rabbits and using their spinal cords to infect other rabbits, I have built a stronger, more virulent form of rabies.

"I did it by using *human guinea pigs for rabbits*. And that's all you are, Mr. Wentworth, my fine bragging Spider, a human guinea pig. Sometime during the night, your man, Ram Singh, will have his first seizure. He will bite you and give you the disease, for that is part of the system I have evolved. The virus is stronger if communicated by the teeth instead of with the needle. And that is why I have stripped you, to make the biting easier."

THE MAN threw back his misshapen, ugly head and laughed his cracked shrill laughter. It was the mirth of a madman, no doubt of that, but a crafty mad man. The man's hideous body and face, the dimly lighted room of cages with its suffering, dying prisoners, the cries of the maniac in the next cell combined to make a scene of incredible horror.

The madman's laughter mounted to a high-pitched note and broke. "So you do not like the idea of being the guinea pig of Dern Bierkson? Well, others have not liked it, but it has done them no good. Shall a guinea pig challenge a scientist?"

Chuckling to himself he walked toward the narrow exit door that squeezed in between two cages and there he lifted his voice, calling, "Jacques!" He shuffled with his queer bent gait back to Wentworth's cage. He could not seem to satiate himself with gloating over these new captives of his. Presently the narrow door opened and a man edged his broad shoulders sidewise through the door. He had a chest like a keg, this one, covered by a tight blue jersey and upon his bead was a cocky cap of wool. A heavy pistol tapped against his thigh as he swaggered up behind Dern Bierkson.

Bierkson jabbed a bony hand at the cage of the Negro. "This guinea pig is ripe for the picking, Jacques," he said in his snarling, harsh voice. "Pick it up and bring in the new specimen."

The burly man in the blue jersey nodded his round head, shifted a cud of tobacco to the other cheek and spat an inches long stream.

The man stared at him, winked, and walked to the cage of the Negro. "Shoot me, too," begged the man diagonally across from Wentworth. He had a two-day growth of red beard upon his cheeks. His hands were gnarled. "Shoot me, you son of a pig and dry-uddered camel, you…" he lapsed into the French of the gutters, heaped filth upon the perverted old scientist and his man, but both ignored him. The pistol was thrust close to the bars. One shot blew the heart out of the Negro. His harsh breathing choked off and the gate clanged open. With a single heave, the blue-jerseyed one hoisted the Negro giant's body to his shoulders.

"Remember," old Bierkson snarled after him, "bring in that other one at once!" He turned toward Wentworth, massaging his bony bands. "This is a little surprise I have for you. I hope you will appreciate it properly."

Wentworth felt tension grow in his chest, felt his pulse become hard and pounding. What new infamy had this madman committed? He clenched his fists at his side, then a curse tore from his lips and he snatched frantically through the bars for the bent old fiend. But the man dodged him with a surprising nimbleness and mocking, shrill laughter.

Wentworth gripped the bars, gripped them and choked down the wrath that was strangling him with hot hands of hate. The thin white scar upon his right temple throbbed. He stared at the door that had swung open a little way to give him a glimpse of the new "human guinea pig" that stood beyond, and now flung wide to admit the swaggering, cocky executioner and his prisoner.

The prisoner was a woman whose clothing had been stripped from her except for a chemise of pale green satin that reached half way down her round white thighs and upward to cover her breasts. Except for that single scanty garment she was naked. The Men crowded against their bars. The woman hung her head.

"Bring her here! Bring her here!" snarled Bierkson. "I have a particular friend of hers for her to meet."

A friend! Wentworth had seen only that the new prisoner was a woman. But a friend! Good God in heaven, could they have captured....

The girl was thrust before the cage. Slowly she raised her head of clustering chestnut curls. Her blue eyes met Wentworth's. He grasped the bars and fury sent the blood buzzing in his ears.

"Nita!" he cried hoarsely. "Oh, God!"

The leering high laughter of Bierkson mocked them.

"Nita indeed!" he sneered. "Do guinea pigs have names?"

CHAPTER 16
FOR HUMANITY!

WHILE THE mad scientist laughed in fiendish glee, while the barking breath of the doomed men sounded mournfully in their ears, Nita van Sloan lifted her head proudly, looked into Wentworth's eyes and smiled.

"Hello, Dick," she said quietly.

Wentworth fought down the horror that surged within him. If she did not know of the hell ahead, he would protect her from it as long as possible. He compelled his lips to smile.

"Delightful to see you again," he said cheerfully. "These slumming parties make one appreciate one's advantages more, don't you think?"

Each carefully ignored the enforced nudeness of the other. Wentworth was thankful that the dim lighting of the place partly concealed Nita and himself. It stirred blind anger within him to see the brutal hands of Nita's captor gripping her soft white arms.

"I understand I'm to be a neighbor of yours for a while," Nita went on in her carefully casual voice.

"Next door," Wentworth nodded.

The man twitched Nita from before Wentworth's cage as if she had been a toy, thrust her through the door and slammed it shut with a dull ringing clang.

"A damned shame, Professor," he grunted, "to waste a pretty piece like her on your fool experiments. You might at least wait...."

"Out of here, vermin!" Bierkson spat. He struck at Jacques with a hand in which metal glinted and the man cried out in mortal fear and darted to the door in panic. The bent old man turned, stared at Nita.

"There is something in what Jacques says, at that," he cackled, "and if I were younger... Listen, my child, it is only tonight that you must sleep alone. Tomorrow I shall allow your lover to enter the cage with you. How much these others would give for the chance!" His voice turned gloating. "But you will not welcome your lover this time, my dear, for during this night his servant will go mad and bite him and when he comes to you the virus of hydrophobia will already be hot within his veins! You understand, my sweet one!

"I have been longing ever since this experiment started to try the virus on a woman. I have a theory that it will develop even more rapidly in a woman and strike even more swiftly when her—when yours, it is, my dear—spinal cord is cut out and used to spread the madness.

"But I hadn't told you, had I, sweet one, what your purpose is? You are just a guinea pig, just a guinea pig to spread the hydrophobia for Brent!"

WENTWORTH CAUGHT at that phrase. It was a confirmation of all that he had thought. Brent was behind this business. The mad old scientist was simply a pawn in the wild and terrible scheme.

"It is a pity I could not have had you a few days sooner," Bierkson maundered on. "I would like to use your spinal cord for tonight's attack on Gary. It is the climax of Brent's plans.

131

Would it not be an honor to participate, even if only vicariously?

"After last night, Brent will issue no more, warnings, he will only attack. With such tactics, there is no reason why Brent can't master the whole country as he has a few towns, no reason why he can't take over Washington, the entire country. Then, what human guinea pigs I should have! All the world through all the ages would ring with my fame. I could solve the mystery of every disease!"

A man poked his head in at the narrow door across the room. "Professor, it's the chief calling about tonight."

Bierkson grumbled "All right," looked about him as if he regretted for a moment having to leave his guinea pigs, then shambled on across the room. Wentworth pressed against the bars of Nita's cell and whispered her name. Her hand touched his.

"Don't let what Bierkson said worry you," Wentworth whispered. "We can be out of here in five minutes any time were left alone that long."

"I wasn't worried," said Nita calmly. "I knew you'd find a way out for us."

Wentworth laughed softly. "If only I had as much confidence in myself as you have in me!" he exclaimed. "Is it night or day, Nita?"

"It's late afternoon," she told him.

An exclamation escaped Wentworth. "And Gary is to be attacked tonight! Judging from what Bierkson said, the city won't be warned at all. Lord, it's a massacre! It is not alone ourselves we must save. It is an entire city!"

He bent over and from between the great toe of his left foot and the one next to it, he slipped a sliver of steel which had been secured there with flesh colored tape. In a stride he had reached the door and bent over the heavy lock. It was a simple fastening, but Wentworth's tool was not the most efficient, and working as he must by thrusting both arms through the bars and reaching at full length over the solid sheet of steel that protected the lock, it was slow work.

Twice he was forced to stop when he thought he heard footsteps, but finally the lock clicked back and he pushed open the gate of his cell. He sprang instantly to Nita's door and bent to the task. It was simpler now that he had opened one lock, now that he could manipulate without straining his arms in awkward positions. A moment later, her door also clicked open and Wentworth spun toward the exit from the room of the human guinea pigs, Nita and Ram Singh behind him.

A deep voice rasped out from the opposite cells. "Either you take me with you, or I'll yell a warning."

Wentworth jerked his head that way, but did not slow his swift stalking.

"I'm going to get the keys if I can," he rapidly told the man. "If I waited to pick all those locks; none of us could escape."

The man stared with narrowed eyes as the three stole on toward the door. "You're lying," he cried out hoarsely. "You're lying. Help!" he shouted. "They're getting away!"

Wentworth reached the door in a bound, knocked it open

with his shoulder and dived to the floor beyond. Jacques was charging across the room with drawn gun. He snapped a shot but the swift dive confused him and he missed.

Before he could fire again, Wentworth sprang from a crouch, thudding into the man's middle with his shoulder, sending him reeling backward. His fingers locked about the man's gun wrist twisting shrewdly.

With an oath, Jacques dropped the weapon and wrapped arms like steel cable about Wentworth. No chance here to match science against brawn. Now it was muscle against muscle. Wentworth felt the arms close like the knives of the iron lady about him, bruising sinews, crunching joints. Peering over the man's shoulder, he saw a huddled bunch of other men burst into the room with daylight behind them. To their left a door flung open and the professor in a white surgical apron, a scalpel in his hand stood outlined in white glare from an operating lamp. They were trapped by an overwhelming force!

WENTWORTH HAD only seconds when he might escape. Now he battled a single man. Though that one was powerful as a Greek wrestler, his strength would be as nothing compared with the combined force of those others approaching warily even now from the doorway. He flung a glance about, seeking the soldier prisoner. He might help them. No soldier was in sight. No help but in himself. His chest laboring, Wentworth panted out a few clipped words in Hindustani—then a strange thing happened.

His breath became hoarse in his throat so that he seemed almost to bark with each exhalation, his jaws began to champ and snap, and his eyes glaring wide, he lunged for the throat of Jacques, baring his teeth like a dog. Horror and fright twisted the face of the man. Wentworth's teeth struck his throat, gouged into the flesh. Jacques screamed.

He snapped his arms from his prisoner and whirled to flee.

"La Rage!" he cried hoarsely. "He have hydrophobia!"

They scattered, screaming.

"Fools!" the bent old professor shouted from the doorway. "It is a trick! He hasn't got hydrophobia!"

He darted to rally his men, slashing wildly with the scalpel. Ram Singh plunged toward them now, teeth snapping as Wentworth's did. The professor lunged into his path, thrust the scalpel at him. A brown arm shot out and pinioned his old, stringy wrist, twisted the surgical knife free. A blow and Dern Bierkson slammed against the wall and collapsed.

Jacques, with Wentworth clinging to his back, smashed into the men. He went through it and out into the open, carrying two others with him. Ram Singh's cries of triumph were sharp, and at each cry a man groaned and collapsed with razor-sharp steel burning his vitals. A moment the huddle at the door lasted, then the battle was over. Ram Singh and Wentworth panted side by side, two naked men, one brown, one as bronzed as an Indian.

In Ram Singh's hand was a bloody scalpel. In Wentworth's was Jacques' heavy revolver. He raised it and fired once and Jacques, sprinting for a nearby house, stumbled. His feet hit the ground awkwardly, toes digging.

From the long low building toward which he had darted,

other men darted out. Guns were in their hands. They spotted the naked men in the doorway and ran toward them.

Wentworth felt a touch on his shoulder, a soft hand, and jerked his head about. Nita stood just behind him.

"The hangar!" Wentworth panted. "The plane that brought you?"

"To your left," Nita said swiftly, and catching her hand, Wentworth darted that way. "Around this building," she directed. Ram Singh streaked beside them.

From the men behind, shouts rang out. The three fugitives whirled the corner, saw the hangar a hundred feet away.

"Ram Singh!" Wentworth shouted. "Start the plane, get Nita in. Come for me!" He released Nita's hand. "Run!"

THEY RACED toward the hangar. Wentworth flung flat on the ground and waited with pistol leveled, a smile twisting his mouth corners.

A man slammed around the house corner and blazed Away at the hangar. The man cursed and slapped his feet down hard in a pounding run and Wentworth knew Nita and Ram Singh had reached cover. He held his fire. In the dusk, the man overlooked the bronze body of the Spider stretched upon the ground. He saw him when he was within fifty feet and a frightened cry jerked from his lips. He threw up his gun. Three other men piled around the corner in a bunch.

Wentworth fired calmly. His first bullet drilled the forehead of the nearest man before he could shoot. At the flash of his pistol, the others loosed a wild fusillade. Lead whined high above him. One bullet spewed dirt into his face. Wentworth fired twice more carefully and two men were hurled into bloody death. The fourth fled. His cries, rallying other men, were shrill. Behind Wentworth the plane roared.

Wentworth sprang up and raced toward his fallen foes, snatched up the pistol of the first man he had shot, dashed to the corner of the building where two more guns lay. He threw a swift glance over the quadrangle between the buildings. A dozen men were charging across it with guns glinting in their hands.

The sound of the plane behind him had steadied to an even, drumming bellow. The hollow note caused by the hangar was gone and he knew Ram Singh or Nita had taxied it out into the open. Wentworth loosed a telling burst of lead, slid to the cover of the building.

Swiftly, while his pursuers were slowed, he sprang to a window and scanned the laboratory's interior. He saw the dissecting table, cages of beasts, the door to the pen of madmen. But nowhere did he see the soldier he hoped to save. Had the professor been bluffing?

Wentworth frowned. He could wait no longer. He whirled, flung back his head and sprinted for the plane. As he neared, it wheeled, and he sprang to the right wing, seizing the edge of the forward cockpit. Instantly the roar of the motor deepened as it was given full throttle. It trundled out onto the field.

Wentworth turned his back to the hurricane of the slipstream, clinging with his right hand, a revolver in his left. A bunched rush of men swiveled the corner of the old professor's building. The flickering small flame of a machine gun danced in the deepening darkness. The plane seemed glued to the ground. It was intended to carry only two and the extra weight made it loggy. There was no wind. It would take a long run to take off—and tall trees crowded close to the edge of the field.

Wentworth steadied his gun with a flexed arm to counteract the heavy jouncing of the ship as it rose slowly. The trees reared before them like a cliff. The propeller clawed the air with a thin scream, the engine labored. Death gibbered at them from those back trees.

WENTWORTH SHOT a glance downward. There was seventy-five feet of space beneath. Those trees, less than fifty feet ahead.... Wentworth thrust his head toward the back cockpit, recognized Nita's white, tense face behind the controls. "Dive and bank!" Wentworth shouted.

The moan of wind through its wire stays mounted to a howl and Nita dove and whirled in a sharp right bank, dropping the wing on which Wentworth stood, so that his weight helped there, too. The breeze was light. It scarcely stirred the tops of the trees, their undercarriage almost touched.

Fighting slowly upward, they swung off in a wide arc southward. Wentworth, crouching on the wing, peered downward seeking land marks, spotted a L-shaped lake a mile to the west where the faint last rays of the sun still lingered. He straightened then. The night air was sharp at this altitude, and Wentworth welcomed the flying suit that Ram Singh held out to him. He climbed into it before he squeezed into the cockpit.

He twisted and cupped his hands to shout to Nita, "Brown-lee!" He saw her head nod and saw her arm, outlined black against the sky, pointing off to the southward and down. Wentworth peered where she pointed. Brilliant white lights from high lamps shone down upon an unpainted wooden house. As he watched, a wave of men rushed across a clearing toward the building. A few fell, but the rest charged on. They reached the house and a group of them began battering at the door.

Wentworth jerked his head about, and Nita nodded again. Good God in heaven! That was Professor Brownlee's laboratory and it was being stormed by men! That could mean only one thing. The Master of the Hordes had located his work shop and was bent on thwarting his shrewd work. Wentworth felt a blow on his shoulder and, turning about, leaned far back to catch Nita's shouted words.

"Brownlee... finished... job."

Brownlee had finished... Wentworth clenched his fist and struck it upon the side of the cockpit. Professor Brownlee had found a way to stop the Hordes, Nita meant. And in the hour of his final triumph, in the hour when Wentworth had discovered the hiding place of the Hordes themselves, Professor Brownlee was being struck down!

CHAPTER 17
BROWNLEE'S JOB

DESPERATELY WENTWORTH fought to find a way out while the plane roared over the last, few miles to Professor Brownlee's laboratory. The men still battered at the door. One fell writhing as he watched, shot from within. There were five of their number stretched on the I ground now. They were not having too easy a conquest.

A sudden smile lighted Wentworth's face. He began to fumble through the pockets of the flying suit and found a piece of paper. Ram Singh's pockets yielded a stub of pencil. While the Hindu held a match in his cupped hands, Wentworth scribbled a dozen words.

He tied the paper to a wrench, signaled Nita to circle low and lower until they were flashing through the white glow of the floodlights from Professor Brownlee's place. Twice they swung through the light and Wentworth waved an arm to the men. Two darted out with rifles raised then paused. Finally they waved a hesitant greeting back to him.

Then Wentworth threw the message to them.

Once more under Nita's hand the plane circled into the darkness, then swooped again. Wentworth waved again.

Three of the men were clustered over the note. They glanced up and as the ship flashed toward the night again, one waved his arm and nodded his head violently in assent. Nita shot the ship upward and they droned off straight away from the scene and, out of hearing of the men, circled for a half hour, then they returned and set the plane down in Professor Brownlee's front yard by the illumination of the flood lights.

The ship stopped with its propeller slicing the air at the laboratory's doorstep. Wentworth sprang down, his hands high. He stood in the bright focus of the lights. There was a shout within, then the door Hung wide and a short, erect little man bounced out onto the porch and clasped Wentworth in his arms.

"The papers said they had you!" he cried.

Wentworth grinned, turned back to the plane and helped Nita, bare-footed, but garbed as he was in a flying suit like white dungarees, to the ground. She threw her arms about the beaming little professor.

"I thought they had you sure," she said, "but Dick threw some sort of note down to them and they left in a hurry. I don't know what he could have written."

Wentworth smiled wryly, striding toward the house. "I just wrote them to leave and protect Bierkson."

"But why should they obey you?"

"They recognized the plane as one of their own and the note was signed 'Brent,'" he said, and was inside at the telephone.

Nita looked at Professor Brownlee. "There never was anyone like him, my dear," said the professor, and together they, followed by the stern-faced Ram Singh, went into the white cottage.

Wentworth's sharp voice was ringing through the room. "Yes, General Lansing, there can be no doubt about it.

They're attacking Gary tonight. In less than an hour, if you'll shoot my Northrup up here"—he gave him the location of Professor Brownlee's laboratory—"I'll be with you. Warn the Army men. I'll be flying the red Northrup."

WENTWORTH SIGNALED the operator again, turned to the professor while he waited. "Nita said you had finished a your job, Professor. Could you figure a gas such as I suggested?" The operator's answer interrupted and Wentworth said into the mouthpiece, "Saginal police, please. Yes, in a hurry," and turned back to the professor.

"Gas, it is, Dick," Brownlee told him. "Your hunch was good, but I couldn't figure a gas that would kill the animals and not the men. However I have a narcotic gas that will keep so close to the ground—it's twice as heavy as air—that it should not affect men at all."

Wentworth nodded and turned to the phone. "The chief, please, and at once. It's important… That's good work, Professor. Better than my plan because it's safer… Hello, Chief? Chief Gallet? This is Richard Wentworth, attached to the Department of justice. Oh, I see. Well, I've escaped from the criminals and I know where their headquarters are." He described the L-shaped lake and the location of Dern Bierkson's gruesome laboratory. "Three hours! But good Lord, can't you use planes? They'll all be gone before you get there if it takes three hours. Very well, do your best. And when you get there look out for mad beasts— and mad men!"

He slapped up the receiver. "Says there aren't any planes to be had. Government's taken them all." He strode to the middle of the low, crudely furnished room and stood on braced bare feet. His flying suit, open at the throat, showed the tight bunched muscles of his chest.

"Professor," he said crisply, "please have your men load a couple of carboys of your gas into the plane out front. When the Northrup comes through from Hurzon, have all it can carry put aboard." He nodded, and the professor hurried from the room. "Nita, any idea who engineered your capture?"

"I went for a walk in the garden and felt myself growing drowsy, Before I could cry out, it had me, I woke up in the plane."

Wentworth nodded, "Wait here until I come back with this plane, then you and Ram Singh fly back to Healy's home. Have Healy arrested at once. Ram Singh, on your life, guard the *missie sahib!*"

"*Han, sahib!*" Ram Singh bowed swiftly. "But, master, if the hydrophobia, seizes me, I shall kill myself instantly so that the *missie sahib* need not fear."

Wentworth's forehead knotted in a frown. "Did you have a chance to burn the wound before you were captured?"

Ram Singh thrust forward his lean brown arm, showing a scabbed and clean wound on his forearm.

"I used the gun powder from two cartridges, and a match, *sahib,*" he said, stony-faced. "And I gave myself the second injection as soon as you left."

"How many hours after you were captured was that other wound on your arm made?" Wentworth asked.

"It is now forty hours, *sahib.*"

The incubation period of the Horde Master's virus was around forty hours! At any moment now the dread madness might seize upon Ram Singh, the faithful. There was a heaviness upon Wentworth. Many times in the years they had been together these two had braved death, had fought to save the other. Many times they had battled insuperable odds and won. But this was a thing that could not be fought. Unless the serum took hold before advanced symptoms set in, Ram Singh had absolutely no chance to recover.

Wentworth crossed, slow-footed to the table where stood a pitcher and a glass. His face was cut by sharp lines, and his eyes were stony.

"Drink a glass of water, Ram Singh."

Casual words! Yet if Ram Singh tried to do so simple a thing as drink a glass of water and failed; if his effort brought his breath harshly from his mouth; if it closed his throat with paroxysmic spasms, there was only one thing for him to do—suicide, the knife!

RAM SINGH realized these things as well as Nita and Wentworth who watched him. He had seen what the mere sound of water did in that hell that Bierkson ruled, yet he walked with an utterly impassive face to the table. His hand reaching for the pitcher and glass were steady as a rock. Wentworth's eyes were fixed on Ram Singh's face, on his throat.

The margin of anti-rabic injection had been much less than prescribed, but the serum he had used was not one that had been widely experimented with. He was not sure what its effect would be. In addition to that, the serum was battling with germs of a more virulent type than ever before had been known to man, thanks to the intensification of the disease accomplished by Bierkson and his human guinea pigs. There was no way of telling what might happen.

Ram Singh had stood well the sight and the sound of water, but could he drink?

Slowly, Ram Singh raised the glass to his lips. His eyes were fixed upon it rigidly and despite his iron control, there was the dawn of horror in their depths. God above, was Ram Singh mad, or was it merely the uncertainty…?

The glass touched his lips. He tilted back his head, opened his mouth. Slowly, smoothly he drank to the last drop!

Nita's pent-up breath burst from her in a deep sigh. Wentworth realized that her nails had bitten into the flesh of his hand. He strode to where Ram Singh stood beside the table and seized his hand.

"Stout fella!" he said heartily. The serum he had given this man at the risk of his own life had taken hold, had immunized him against the dread rabies.

Professor Brownlee hustled back into the room. "The plane will be ready in two minutes," he said rapidly. "I have the gas both in carboys and wax bombs. I put both in the plane."

"Fine!" Wentworth nodded. "Nita, when you get to Healy's home, be sure you order his arrest immediately. If you can't get it on any other grounds, swear that he assisted in your abduction. I'm going back to put my seal on the foreheads of those lads I killed at the laboratory," he said. "I didn't have my cigarette lighter before but the Professor always keeps a spare for me."

He received the lighter, a revolver and ammunition, canvas sneakers for his feet.

"If I'm not back in three quarters of an hour," he said, "do these things, Ram Singh, fly to Gary and use the gas the professor tells you. Nita, you'll have to use a car to Healy's home— if I don't come back!"

He grinned at them all from the doorway, strode out into the night.

CHAPTER 18
MADMAN'S JUSTICE

WENTWORTH'S PLANS for holding Bierkson and his men until police could reach the hidden laboratory were vague. Roaring through heavy night air on the short hop that separated Brownlee's place from that hell-hole of the mad scientist, he swiftly reviewed the battle ahead. If the police had got under way instantly at his call, they still would be fully two and a half hours from the spot when Wentworth reached there. And he could not tarry. Within an hour he must be speeding northward to Gary. Without him, the defense would crumple as it had at Hurzon before the assault of the Mad Hordes.

Eyes questing for the glint of water that would reveal the L-shaped lake which was his only landmark, Wentworth scanned the black earth below. It would be three o'clock before the moon rose tonight. The glimmer of the stars was faint and aloof. Fifteen minutes of swift flight and the distant black reflection of water gave him his location. Swinging in a wide circle, he spotted white buildings below.

He swooped a grenade in his hand. His mouth shut in a hard line. That bomb should blow to bits those vile laboratories below, spatter the henchmen of the Hordes over the landscape. He jerked his head in negative. Though he held little scruple about destroying these vermin who had loosed death and desolation upon the country, he still did not wish to kill those suffering men penned in Bierkson's prison of horrors. Doomed they might be, but they were innocent of wrong-doing and some might be saved. No, there must be another way.

He swung wide and hurled the bomb—into the woods. Circling again, he saw lights prick out in the buildings below. Searchlights swept the woods and swung upward to stripe the sky with light. Wentworth picked up his microphone.

"Turn off those searchlights or I'll blow every one of you to hell," he boomed through the loudspeaker.

Flame spat upward from rifles, flickered from machine guns.

"The Spider speaking," Wentworth thundered down at them. "Last warning. Turn off the lights or be blown up. Listen, fools, and obey. All your secrets are known. Brent had got all the wealth. He told your secrets and skipped. Brent has betrayed you. Brent didn't want you to share the gold. He has betrayed you."

Slanting downward in a propeller speeded dive, Wentworth hurled a grenade that blew the searchlight to bits.

The upward spitting flame of gunfire lessened, dwindled to a petty popping. Wentworth swung lower, saw the door of the laboratory and prison flung open, saw the bent old figure of the mad doctor of hydrophobia in a blazing oblong of white light. It poured out into the night and stretched his black shadow on the earth. He gesticulated like a mediaeval priest exorcising devils. Men trooped up to him and Wentworth saw their hands flying as they argued, magnified hugely, by their shadows.

A man stepped close to the professor and struck at him. The old madman reeled backward and the door slammed.

But it was shut only a moment, then it flung wide again, and the men fled from its light as from a physical blow. Their thin screams pierced even through the roar of the engine. Naked men stood in the light-flooded doorway. Wentworth knew them. They were Bierkson's human guinea pigs. Their jaws gnashed in the frenzy of hydrophobia!

THEY STREAMED from the brightly lighted doorway out into the blackness. A half dozen at first, then more and more until two score had poured out into the night, bounding crazily to the attack. Some fell from the scattering gun fire of the gangsters, but others survived to pursue. Behind them other hordes rushed, loosed by the enraged Bierkson; dogs and cats and scampering, vicious bats.

Wentworth swooped and smacked three bombs into the midst of the animals. The ripping grenades dug huge craters in the earth, blew the rush of hordes out of existence. No way to tell what was happening in the blackness below, how the gangsters' guns served them in their battle with the mad Frankensteins they had created. The hydrophobic men outnumbered their masters two to one. Many of the beasts, too, had escaped the bombs. They would strike naked men and gangsters alike.

Wentworth's bombs had not been out of mercy to the gang, but to avert the spread of the plague through wild animals and domestic cattle that these beasts could infect. He dropped one more grenade as a final scattering of the hordes shambled from the door.

Scarcely had the blast rumbled into silence when the hunched old figure of the insane experimenter threw its distorted shadow out upon the bomb-torn earth. He shook a scrawny fist at the night, stepped from the doorway. Suddenly he whirled.

As he spun, a naked white giant stepped from the blackness and flung upon him. He did not strike with his hands and feet, did not wield gun or knife. He seized the professor by his twisted shoulder. He pushed back his head with violent hand and sank his teeth into Bierkson's throat!

The old man's arms slowed. His hands beat feebly against the hunched shoulders of the giant, then one dropped and fumbled in his clothing. It jerked up, and steel glinted in its grasp. Bierkson slapped the steel against the side of the giant's neck!

Blood that glistened blackly spurted where the steel touched, but the naked madman gave no other sign of the wound. The professor's old hand reached straight up to heaven, stiffened, and dropped. For moments longer the naked giant held his prey, then he dropped Bierkson to the ground like a broken toy. The man threw back his head. Good Lord! The man was laughing! For a long minute he stood like that, then his knees sagged. He dropped to them and slumped slowly down upon his face.

A shudder shivered over Wentworth. Never before had he seen death as horrible as that, death beneath the teeth of a mad man! But it was just, just! The professor had died at the jaws of a man he had deliberately infected.

Once more Wentworth reached into the divided compartment before him and took out grenades. Sweeping upward and diving at top speed across the laboratory he sent two bombs smashing against the roof, raced and whanged two against the sleeping quarters of the gangsters.

Filled with the tense need for speed, for clean pure air to sweep the horror from his brain, Wentworth sent the plane roaring with throttle wide open back to the laboratory of Professor Brownlee.

Whatever happened at Gary, the fiend who had fathered the fearful hordes was dead. His henchmen were scattered into the night with raging madmen on their trails, with the shadows, full of mad beasts whose teeth meant death with police racing to take them. These were destroyed, but Brent, the Master of the Hordes, survived.

But first must come Gary!

Gary. Thousands of lives were at stake there. And all depended on Professor Brownlee and his gas. The technique of battling the hordes had been improved, but Wentworth knew it would not suffice. God grant he could reach Gary in time!

Wentworth swung in a fast circle over the laboratory, spotted his scarlet Northrup in the edge of the shadows near the house and shot his ship down to a slam bang landing, side-slipping almost to a standstill, straightening out for a three pointer that did not roll a dozen feet. He sprang to the earth, darted toward the house, then abruptly he whirled and sprinted, toward the Northrup.

A man with a gun crouched in the shadows of the open door. Wentworth's grin was a fearful thing. That one man might doom Gary's thousands!

CHAPTER 19
ON TO GARY!

A S WENTWORTH swerved from his direct path to the house and spurted toward the safety of the night, the man sprang into view and blasted singing lead after him. Wentworth's grin was mocking, his eyes hard, and ugly. The man was a fool. But the first knowledge he had of his insanity was the Spider's lead slamming like a trip-hammer into his chest, driving him back against the door-jamb. That was as far as his sensations went. When he hit the floor he was dead.

A foot on the Northrup's wing, Wentworth vaulted to the cockpit. His feet struck something that yielded. A voiceless groan wheezed from it. Wentworth's hand leaped forward and seized hold of a man. The man's flesh was cold beneath his hand. The thick stickiness of blood oozed between his fingers. The man was dead. Wentworth's feet striking his chest had driven out his breath.

By the feeble light of the stars, Wentworth examined the body. The man was an army pilot. A dozen bullets had torn through his head and chest.

Wentworth looked further and found he had contrived to wreck the throttle of the plane before he had died. Wentworth knew then the reason for this attack. These killers were men of the Hordes seeking to escape. They could not be those who had fled from the Camp of the Human Guinea Pigs. Perhaps these were some of that group he had tricked into abandoning the attack on Brownlee's place, some who had lingered behind and seen the plane they thought their own land Brownlee's friends.

Gently, Wentworth eased the corpse of the soldier from the cockpit, lowered it to the ground, then he reached for his sub-machine guns. Their compartment was well hidden and he did not think—ah, here was one. He drew it out, a compact instrument of sudden death, and, snapping on a drum of ammunition, he crept toward the house.

A pistol spat at him from a window and Wentworth ripped a burst of sizzling lead. The pistol was not discharged again. A shadow in the doorway. Wentworth jerked up the machine gun, then halted, cold horror trembling down his spine. The shadow in the doorway was Nita!

"Go ahead and shoot," a man's voice jeered, and Wentworth saw its owner crouched behind Nita. "Go ahead. You crack down just once more and I'm going to blow a hand off the girl. Just by way of warning...."

Wentworth began to back slowly toward the darkness.

"Stand still!" the man snarled. "You stand right there until… Herb! Come out here and take this punk. He's got a typewriter, so watch him."

A man stepped boldly into sight, sidled along the house. Why were they taking so much trouble to capture him alive, Wentworth wondered. A single shot would put him out of the picture.

"Don't hurt him, Herb," the man behind Nita warned. "He's got to take us away from here!"

So that was it! They had no one with them who could fly a

plane and did not know that Nita and Ram Singh were both excellent pilots. Wentworth held out the machine gun to the man called Herb and docilely allowed himself to be herded toward the laboratory.

It would not be difficult to overpower this man beside him, but escape without Brownlee's narcotic gas would be futile, the sacrifice of Nita that would be involved would be vain. No, he must allow himself to be taken an apparently willing captive, and trust to his keen brain. But delay meant the difference between life and death to thousands!

TREADING LIGHTLY with alert muscles and brain, Wentworth was taken up to the porch with a machine-gun muzzle at his spine. Nita smiled at him wanly and he flung a swift glance about the room, saw Brownlee and Ram Singh tied and glimpsed the man behind Nita, a round-faced pallid man, with hairless eyelids like a snake's.

"I thought that would fix you up," he said in an oily voice.

Wentworth's glinting eyes fixed on his forehead. He seemed slightly amused. The man frowned.

"Listen, bozo," he snarled, "you're going to fly us away from here and do it quick."

Wentworth's eyes did not swerve.

"Get out of the way, Herb," the moon faced man snarled. "This baby is going to take a fall."

He took two strides forward and slashed sideways with the barrel of his gun at Wentworth's head. The head wasn't there. The man spat out a curse and stepped in close. Wentworth caught the wrist as the man struck and flung himself backward.

At the breaches in the fence Wentworth dropped the gas

carboys—but did not wait to see the Hordes wilt.

Wentworth, flopping on his back, dug both feet into the man's belly as he hit and heaved upward. The gunman, crunched down on his head.

Wentworth rolled to his right, like a log, lunging down an incline. The machine-gun bullets Herb loosed ploughed the floor so close behind him, that Wentworth's flying suit jerked with the flicking tug of the lead. Herb yelled as Wentworth slammed against his legs. The machine gun bit off its chatter and Herb attempted to dance backward.

He hit the wall hard kicked at Wentworth. Wentworth sprang up and smashed a right to the jaw. Herb went to sleep.

A knife from his pocket and Wentworth had freed the three prisoners.

"They got us when the Northrup landed," Brownlee explained shamefacedly. "We went out to meet the pilot."

"Where are your assistants?" Wentworth rapped out.

Brownlee's face grew bleak.

"Dead," he said briefly. "They tried to shoot it out with those four."

Wentworth jerked the last rope free, bound his prisoner. "And the gas, Professor?" he asked over his shoulder.

"About a third made," the Professor called as he ran to his laboratory.

Time, time! The fates seemed to conspire against Gary. For the professor must work alone on the gas since the assistants who knew the details of Its manufacture were dead.

Wentworth finished binding the gangster. "Ram Singh!" he

called. "The throttle of the Northrup is smashed. It must be fixed at once!"

The Hindu crossed the room in two bounds, plunged out the door.

"Nita, you'll have to take off alone," Wentworth told her swiftly. "It's more important than ever that you reach the Healy home and have him placed under arrest. I may fail at Gary. If I do...."

HE BROKE off and ran to the laboratory to help Professor Brownlee, waving a hand as Nita also raced to the door.

Wentworth was still binding the strings of the rubber laboratory apron about him when the motor of the plane blasted into the night, steadied and hurtled off into the blackness. Nita was on the way! He turned to Professor Brownlee, already bent like a sorcerer above a steaming cauldron from which brown acrid gas rose.

"Tell me what to do, Professor."

Through dragging hours, the two labored over mixtures that simmered from self-generated heat, over brews that steamed and smoked, over others that frosted the glass they touched.

A bit of dull gray metal dropped into a seething mess popped like a fire cracker along its surface and Professor Brownlee raised a haggard face. The clock registered three minutes of eleven. "One more operation, Dick, and we'll pump it into the cylinders. I've got plenty of those, but damned few bomb shells."

Wentworth nodded grimly, ran to the phone and called General Lansing at Gary. The brigadier's voice crackled in his ear.

157

"I expected you here by now," he barked out. "We've been here only an hour. Oil trench is dug as you suggested. We're expecting the attack any moment."

Wentworth cut in.

"Please detail three planes to rush here at top speed," he asked. "And bring some chemists in them. The planes will have to be small. The landing field won't allow more than two hundred feet run. I can't carry much gas on my Northrup. Wait," he stopped Lansing's nervous interjection and went on. "I can bring all Professor Brownlee was able to manufacture in one batch. As soon as this is finished he'll start another.

"I'll take off in half an hour, be there in another hour. Any sign of attack yet?"

"No, none," Lansing said, then his voice cut off as over the wire came a rumbling vibration.

"What was that?" Wentworth cried.

"That," came General Lansing's grim voice, "was the attack."

He slammed up the receiver.

Another half hour of racing work and the job was finished. Wentworth seized a carboy of gas. Hoisting it to his shoulder, he ran with long, even strides to the Northrup. Ram Singh straightened.

"All is ready now," he said.

"Start the motor and let it warm up," Wentworth snapped out. "Load this carboy in the baggage compartment."

As he whirled back to the house, sprinting, he heard the mounting whine of the compression starter, then the first coughing explosions of the motor. Six carboys they stored in the tail compartment. Two were lashed on each wing close against the fuselage. Ram Singh held another between his knees in the forward cockpit and he was no more than settled when Wentworth sprang in behind him, yanked open the throttle.

THE CARBOYS were cast iron and though their contents were not heavy, they made a terrific load for the Northrup with its limited wing spread to lift on the short run that was possible on this restricted field. At Wentworth's signal, Professor Brownlee put chocks in front of the wheels and Wentworth, foot heavy on the brakes, let them remain until the engines were roaring, full blast.

When he waved his arm and the chocks were jerked free, the Northrup sprang forward. Like a whippet behind a mechanical rabbit. Its dash was swift and violent and Wentworth muscled the ship off the ground with a zoom and a dive and a bounce from swiftly reversed controls.

Wentworth shot a glance at his radium gleaming wrist dial as he wheeled to the northwest. It lacked but twelve minutes of twelve. The attack had been under way twenty minutes, bombs blasting the fences, the Hordes pouring through the breaches, drooling jaws agape. And he was an hour away!

The Northrup, logy with its heavy load, trembled under the throb of its powerful engine, driven at peak speed. The black landscape seemed to crawl beneath them with leaden slowness, despite the better than two hundred mile gait.

Miles of defenses were flung about Gary. The Hordes might attack in a dozen places. A carboy could guard only one entrance for perhaps a half hour. The few wax bombs would take care of another. After that....

Professor Brownlee was already at work on another mixture and help was on the way—a series of black blots against the sky resolved itself into army planes speeding to Brownlee's assistance and Wentworth rocked his wings in salute as he shot past—but at best it would be three hours before another load could start.

He strained his eyes into the northwest. Blue-white pencils of light wrote hieroglyphics across the northwestern sky, then as he watched all winked out but one whose beam cut off and on at space intervals. For a full minute that continued, then it began to flicker in dots and dashes.

Wentworth had requested certain formation and advised against use of radio lest they be overheard. It was less likely the gangs would know Morse.

The message* was:

Seven o'clock wind. Worst breach three clock. Fires low.

That last phrase was ominous. The oil fires that alone sup-

---

* AUTHOR'S NOTE: In military parlance, a seven o'clock wind would be just to the west of south. A breach at three o'clock would be the point due east of a spot in the center of the defenses. The method is primarily for artillery usage and is employed by spotters in telling the men firing the guns the locations of their hits in relation to the target, which is always assumed to be the center of a clock face.

ported that single fence were nearly out. When they flickered
into darkness, the Hordes would pour into the city!

ALREADY WENTWORTH could make out the yellow
rip of fire that girded the city. Minutes dragged past with a
labored slowness that made the plane seem to stand still. At
five miles distance, Wentworth threw the ship into a long dive,
joyfully felt the vibration of his mounting speed. He swept
toward the eastern flank of the city where the message had
indicated the gravest danger.

"Ram Singh," Wentworth spoke into the head-phone set
that linked them, get ready with that carboy. When I throw my
right hand, open the valve and drop for the opening in the
fence. Try to hit just to the south of it."

Lower Wentworth swept until the upturned faces of soldiers,
caged in against the fierce forays of the vampire bats, showed
plainly along the fence. Wentworth could not know, but as the
scarlet plane streaked overhead, a faltering cheer arose. It gained
volume and became a roar of hope. Those men, beleaguered
through hours of weird battling with tiny, fearful foes, saw
salvation. They bent more vigilantly over their guns.

The breach in the fence jerked into view. Wentworth threw
up his hand and a tumbling oblong of black, the carboy of a
gas, spun downward. It struck the hard earth with a fine accuracy that attested Wentworth's good eye and instantly the greasy
dark gas began to coat the earth.

Would the gas operate as Professor Brownlee had promised?
Would it bowl over those Hordes that swept terribly upon the
city, or had his laboratory experiments been too hastily con-

ducted? There had been no opportunity to make tests under identical conditions with these... Two blazing white Very lights burst upon the black night.

Across that patch of light-drenched earth loped the most horrible of all the Hordes, the wolves of the death-branded heads. They plunged into the greasy fog that hugged the earth like a black mobile snow. Wentworth focused his gaze on the gaunt horrible beast that led the pack. Once, twice he dipped into the gas and reared to leap onward. Three more such strides and he would be past the gas!

The third spring faltered. He bounded again, feebly, and his front legs collapsed under him. He kicked, rolled, and lay still. The gray killers behind him did not have his strength. They collapsed before they had twice dipped into the gas.

"Take the controls, Ram Singh, follow the fence!" he ordered and felt the Hindu's hand firm upon the stick. He climbed out on the wing. Black stretches blotted out the flames at intervals now along the fire trench. The oil was failing. Let it fail now!

At three more breaches in the fence, Wentworth dropped the carboys and did not wait to see the Hordes falter and wilt, did not wait to see the spiteful rifle flashes that finished them. With another huge bomb ready, he waited tensely as they raced near the next breach. But, almost on the point of releasing it, he checked. Not an animal was in sight!

CHAPTER 20
THE HUMAN HORDE

WENTWORTH CHECKED the carboy on the verge of tumbling it to the earth. It yanked him off balance and he clung frantically to the fuselage with one hand, the other hanging on to the carboy. That was incredibly precious. A hundred lives might well hinge on saving it—A hundred? A thousand. The plane hit rough air and tilted. The carboy slipped another inch. Wentworth's arm was nearly wrenched from its socket, still he fought to save the carboy through moment after moment of Herculean strain. He gasped out orders to Ram Singh, but the wind whipped the dim words from his lips. The motor drowned the sound. Abruptly the Hindu seemed to sense his master's peril. His lean hand seized Wentworth's. He deliberately rocked the ship to the right so that the carboy's own weight rolled it back on the wing.

Wentworth could not rest. There was no time. He peered downward again. Each breach as he swept over it was brilliantly lighted by Very stars and at one of them did he spot the inrushing Hordes. Had the Master quit the battle so soon? Wentworth jerked his head in negative. That was ridiculous. No, there was some new strategy. His eyes narrowed. He spun to the cockpit where Ram Singh sat.

"Land there!" he shouted and pointed to a cleared space within the line of buildings as they slanted toward it.

Wentworth described a park. With most planes of the Northrup's power, the landing would have been impossible, but

Wentworth's Scarlet ship was equipped with wing slots which gave it a landing speed scarcely forty-five miles an hour. The field was illuminated only by nearby street lights but they knew the direction of the wind and Ram Singh boldly put the ship into a glide. "It jounced once then he snubbed the speeding ship to a halt. Wentworth sprang down and sprinted toward the street.

He spotted a garage, dashed to it and commandeered four cars with drivers. A phone call to General Lansing made, he hopped one of the cars and guided it back to the park, up over the curbing and across level lawns to the plane.

The carboys of gas were speedily loaded on the machines, and, leaving Ram Singh to guard the plane Wentworth raced to Lansing's headquarters. Other cars waited there and, loaded with one carboy each, they sped off into the night.

That accomplished, Wentworth strode into headquarters where General Lansing paced up and down a barren office in which were no chairs and only two tables. On one a map of the city was spread. On the other was a battery of telephones. They kept three men busy and they constantly ran back and forth between the phones and the map where a fourth man made notations and shifted colored pins.

Lansing grunted a greeting to Wentworth, but did not cease his pounding up and down with leather-heeled boots. His long skinny legs flexed at every step.

"You guessed his strategy exactly right. He waited until the plane had passed, then loosed his animals again. With a carboy placed at each breach, we can loose the gas whenever it is needed. Cover all points."

"I want hand bombs for my plane," said Wentworth briefly.

Lansing barked an order at the telephone men, and a man dashed excitedly to the table and removed yellow, red and blue pins and substituted white ones. He ran back to his phone. "The gas is turning the tide," Lansing jerked out. Muscles knotted along his jaw in his excitement. More white pins replaced other colors. An orderly saluted in the doorway.

"Bombs here, sir."

LANSING NODDED and Wentworth stalked out, leaving the general bending over the map, barking occasional orders to the men at the phones. A motorcycle with a sidecar waited outside. Wentworth flung into the car and the driver jerked the machine forward. They passed the next corner at seventy miles an hour. In the floor of the sidecar bombs were wedged tightly. They jostled with the furious speed, almost jounced out as the cycle bounded over the curb.

The stutter of a machine gun ripped out on the quiet air. From the trees beyond the scarlet Northrup a ragged volley of rifle fire answered.

Wentworth knew what this attack meant. Forces of Hordes within the city! But it would be almost impossible to prevent such a thing. The animals themselves could be kept out, and had been, by the ceaseless patrol and inspection of buildings which most industrial towns had instituted on federal advice—inspired by Wentworth—almost from the first day of the plague.

That was the reason it was necessary for the Hordes to make a frontal attack.

If Gary fell, there was an end of resistance to the Hordes. They would run wild over the land, and Brent would reign supreme.

These thoughts coursed through Wentworth's mind as the motorcycle eased up behind the plane. Ram Singh's machine gun fire was careful and accurate. Each flash of a pistol drew his swift lead like a magnet and many fell silent. Wentworth leaned down and with skillful fingers spun loose the wing bolts that held carriage and cycle together. The soldier twisted a surprised head.

"Stay here and load the bombs," Wentworth ordered calmly. He fastened two of the twelve pound bombs to the saddle, forked the motorcycle and sent it rocketing back toward the street. Bullets sped past. A hit on one of those bombs....

The motorcycle bounced into the street and Wentworth whirled toward the position of the enemy. For a moment the firing broke out with redoubled fury. It lasted for thirty seconds, then shut off entirely. Rounding the corner of the park, Wentworth saw a half dozen men dart to an automobile and race away. They continued to fire back at him. Gradually he allowed them to draw away, but never quite lost sight. He knew the tricks of dodge and pursuit too well. Doubling back, twisting and racing through streets all failed. He was always just in sight.

After three-quarters of an hour of that, the auto ducked into a side street near the defense lines and Wentworth, whirling after them, found only a vacant thoroughfare. He halted and slowly surveyed the houses that fronted it. Not one showed a light. There were utterly no signs of occupancy. He propped up the back wheel of his cycle, wedged a bomb beneath his arm, and carried the other gun in his right hand, then, he moved along.

Three quarters of the way down the block, Wentworth halted. Was his imagination playing him tricks or had something moved on that dark cellar stairway? He slipped into deeper shadow and waited, gun poised. For moments, nothing more happened. Then a man's head thrust out into the wan light of the moon; a man's head, then his naked torso, his entire body.

Behind him another man showed and, without warning, the first man whirled and struck at him viciously. The second snapped with his teeth, then others began to push past them out into the street and wander aimlessly toward the soldier's lines. The Horde Master's beasts had failed, so he was loosing human beasts upon the city!

Upon the breast of each man was a brand, *the death's head brand of the Master of the Hordes!*

CHAPTER 21
DEATH AT THE CASTLE

A S IF madness and death were not enough torture to inflict, the Master of the Hordes had submitted these doomed men to the torment of fire merely to satisfy his vanity. And now they were being forced to fight the battle of the Hordes, loosed upon soldiers to terrify them. A branded madman peered for a long moment more into the shadows where Wentworth crouched, then his head swung heavily about and he turned down the street behind the others.

They herded along like mad wolves, striking viciously at one another, never heeding the blows they gave and received. Wentworth trailed them, teeth clamped together, eyes bitter. These men must die, either by the guns of the soldiers or with the strangling torture of rabies gripping their throats.

They were pitiful, these men, and yet they constituted a formidable menace to the safety of the city. The gas would be useless against them. The terrifying threat of naked mad men with death head brands upon their chests might smash the lines and let the Hordes in—

The Human Horde, sixty strong, debauched from the street into the open behind the army's lines and as they walked, flitting black shadows darted blackly across the face of the moon. The mad vampire bats! The Master was piling horror on horror! A gonged warning rang along the lines and men darted beneath wire covers, shields like huge hemispherical rat traps. Gas could not harm the vampires, but when that gonged warning rang out, men could take shelter from their piercing, death-laden teeth.

The naked madmen marched on like troops to battle. Bats struck at them and they tore them apart and flung them to the ground without interest. Wounds mean nothing to the victims of hydrophobia. A shrill shout of warning rang down the line. The soldiers had spotted this new flanking peril. White faces turned fearfully. A naked six-footer stumbled against a soldier's wire cage, snatched at it and hurled soldier and cage to the earth. Another man flung himself snarling upon the soldier, teeth gnashing.

Two men fired as one and the soldier who had fallen prey to the Human Horde sprang to his feet. Still screaming, he fled in panic from the Horde. Bats circled about him like huge lethal mosquitoes. His fear was contagious. Other men dashed in terror from the protection of their cages as the Human Horde rolled on. From beyond the fence, a black line rolled like a drowning wave toward the breach. It was such a force of mad beasts as never before had been loosed.

BENEATH THE white, frightened moon, the charging beasts, the stumbling and murderous naked giants, the soldiers fleeing in panic made a nightmare scene. Cursing himself for his weakness, his moment of pity for these mad killers, Wentworth broke from cover, running heavily with the weight of the bombs upon him. He plunged toward the abandoned posts of the soldiers. In the wake of the bestial hordes he could make out now the vaulting leaps of the death's head wolves, the slinking cats, the scamper of the rodents. On they swept, yet no hand loosed gas to stop them. The last soldier had fled from the horror of his own kind gone mad!

The sound of Wentworth's pounding feet caught the ear of a hulking hydrophobic maniac and he turned awkwardly, lowered his head and charged. Wentworth fired with his unfailing accuracy.

Wentworth ran on, saw others of the Horde turn toward him and shamble to the attack. His face set in a grim, forbidding mask. There was no help for it. These men were innocent tools of the Master, but it was their lives against those of the city's thousands.

Wentworth laid one bomb on the earth, seized the other by its finned tail with both hands and, whirling like a hammer thrower, tossed it a full hundred feet into the midst of the thickest group of the Human Horde. He flung himself flat with the momentum of his swing, felt concussion sweep over him like a black wave. Instantly he was up and racing toward the breach with the one remaining bomb. Bats darted at him, but the Human Horde was wiped out. He snatched up the overturned cage of a soldier who had fled, jerked it over his head, and raced on.

The first of that wave of beasts was almost at the opening of the fence. Wentworth hurled the cage from his shoulders, seized the other bomb and spun in a violent hammer throw. He fell and snatched at the cage again. A bat wheeled toward his throat. He struck it with the wire shield, knocked it aside and ducked beneath the cage. The tearing force of the explosion hurled him flat, wrenched at the wire protector. He clung to it desperately, yanked it over head and neck. A bat fastened its hooks into the shoulder of the thin flying suit. He rolled and ground it into the earth, jerked the cage into position and dashed on.

His bomb had torn a huge crater at the breach, had hurled back the first thick wave of the beasts, but they were closing up again like a tidal wave.

He reached the breach, stared about frantically. Where was the carboy? He searched desperately, finally saw a dull glint of metal half buried by the earth the blast had tossed up. He flung himself upon it, scooping earth backward with both hands like a dog after a bone. He cleared the head of the cylinder, twisted the valve, and the dark greasy waves of the gas spewed out in his face. He jerked upward, reeling, clung to the cage for support. **THROUGH EYES** that were bleary from the narcotic gas, he saw the dark vapor spread over the earth, drift downward into the bomb-hole. The Hordes poured over the outer lip and collapsed in a writhing pile of bodies. The roar of a motor pulled Wentworth's heavy head upward and he saw his scarlet Northrup swish past. He had just consciousness enough left to drop flat before the bombs let go, blowing the unconscious Hordes to atoms. More bombs smashed down. He dragged himself upward with fingers gripping the wires.

Other planes droned through the air now and, his head clearing, staring into the night sky, Wentworth saw three ships in tight formation cross the face of the moon. Three planes! Three had gone to the laboratory of Professor Brownlee. Could they be back with the gas? Wentworth peered like a drunken man at the face of his watch. Three-thirty! It could be the same planes. They swung low and he saw a carboy tumble to the earth, saw black gas spread to reinforce that which he had loosed into the breach.

Wentworth lifted up the cage and staggered back from the lines, back up the long street that was silver on one side and black shadow on the other, back to his motorcycle and at long last to headquarters. General Lansing had three men busy on

171

the telephones, giving out orders, distributing the new carboys of gas.

He took one minute to swing his long legs across to where Wentworth stood, clothing torn, face smeared with blood and earth. He wrung his hand.

"One more time, Wentworth, you have saved the city," he bit out. "That was glorious work there at No. 9 Breach. Got it all by phone. Going to recommend Congressional Medal, Distinguished Service Medal, Legion—but, hell, I forgot. You've already got those things."

He clasped Wentworth's hand once more and flung his long, energy-ridden body back to the phones jerking out orders in monosyllables. Wentworth smiled faintly. Yes, the battle was over, the Hordes turned back. The city was saved, the threat to the nation was broken. But the leader of it all, the ruthless killer who had conceived this fantastic horror and loosed it upon the world remained free and unpunished. The faint smile became thin as a surgeon's scalpel. Work for the Spider!

Wentworth started to go, then turned back. "That soldier sent to follow me at Hurzon—ever hear from him—?"

Lansing nodded. "They found his nude body at the camp in the woods where you sent police."

Wentworth nodded and this time left headquarters, met Ram Singh face to face.

"Good work," Wentworth said curtly. "Tonight's deed will fill your cup with honor for many moons to come, oh, Ram Singh."

Ram Singh's body stiffened with pride, his eyes flashed.

"The glory is yours, *sahib!*"

WENTWORTH CLAPPED him on the back and to-
gether they strode off into the darkness to mount the motorcycle again and speed to the airport and his scarlet Northrup.
Minutes for refueling and they spurted into the air and winged
swiftly off into the southeast. Immediately Wentworth was
busy at his radio. At long last, he raised a Cologne amateur who
got hold of the police for him.

"Has Healy been arrested?" he demanded. "Has Healy been
arrested? Healy arrested?" The answer came back thinly, rasping.
"No. Warrant refused. Warrant refused for Healy."

Wentworth's voice grew harsh and commanding, "I demand
his immediate arrest. Unless you act, I shall see that Washington does. I'll appeal to Washington. Arrest Healy, or I'll call
Washington."

"Call Washington and be damned to you," the police voice
rasped back. "There is no evidence against Healy."

"But, it's absolutely necessary...." Wentworth began. "Hello.
Hello. Helloooo QZB2. Helloooo!"

"Sorry," came back the amateur's thin voice. "He got sore
and left. He got sore and left. He got sore and went away. Sorry."

Wentworth called Washington and demanded and got of-
ficial action after he had explained that all the attacks of the
Hordes were for Healy's profit. "Well get hold of them by phone.
Get them by phone. Order arrest. We'll have Healy arrested!" Washington pledged.

Satisfied, Wentworth relaxed at the controls and let the plane
fly itself with its full terrific speed back toward the Castle. He

would have to land at Cologne and taxi to the Healy home. He might even snatch a moment to wash up before he went there, to wash and get some decent clothing…. With Healy arrested, he could afford a moment of leisure.

He did those things and he took his moment of leisure, and when he reached the Castle, Berthold Healy was stretched upon the floor of his book-lined library with its high single window, his comfortable, homey library that was harsh now with un-shaded electric bulbs. He lay on his back and there was a bullet wound in his right temple.

"He killed himself in here just after we came to arrest him," the sergeant of police said. "He came in here alone and shot himself. Geez, think of him being the brains of that mad-dog gang all the time, and him the biggest man in the country and then some—"

CHAPTER 22
THE MASTER!

WENTWORTH WENT slowly from the room. Outside birds were twittering with the first thrill of the new day, a dawn blush was in the east. Nita met him with outstretched arms. Haggard circles were beneath her glorious eyes, tiny tight lines about her mouth corners. A loose blue negligee draped its heavy silken folds about her.

"I'm glad, Dick, that it ended this way," she said. "For once"— she glanced about her—"the seal of the Spider will not be necessary."

174

Wentworth smiled and kissed her tenderly. "Darling," he said. "I want you to do something for me when we have rested. After Mrs. Healy retires for the evening, go to her room and persuade her to spend the night in your room. Keep her there until I come."

Nita stared up into his face with eyes that once more were darkening with fear.

"Isn't it over, yet, Dick?" her breath caught in her throat.

Wentworth shook his head slowly. "Not yet, my darling. If Mrs. Healy demurs at doing what you wish, tell her it is a matter of life and death—her life and death. And remind her of the walk we all took in the garden."

"The walk in the garden?" Nita said it slowly, but Wentworth only smiled, squeezed the softness of her shoulders and sent her away to rest....

The household was late to retire that night after the naps of the day and Wentworth sat with them casually, his eyes burning with fatigue, but his smile never fading. At long last the women went up and Scarlet and Collins and Wentworth followed them after a drink around. Bidding the others good-night, Wentworth entered his room, but a moment later slipped out and angling across the hall listened a moment at another door that opened into the boudoir of Sybil Healy. He opened the door and went in.

An hour later he left the room and going to Nita's he returned with Sybil Healy beside him to her boudoir. She stared up in bewilderment at his taut, weary face. Once inside the room he left the lights out and secreted her and himself in the dark recesses of a closet whose door he left open. They could see her bed clearly by the dim rose lamp that, heavily shaded, threw a small cone of faint light there.

A woman seemed to be asleep in the bed, a woman with long black hair that streamed over the pillow.

"But I don't understand." Sybil Healy whispered for the twentieth time.

"Just keep thinking about the walk in the garden," Wentworth told her quietly. "Then when the person who is going to enter this room comes in, you will understand. But you must remain silent. Remember, it is yourself that lies in that bed so far as any other person in the world knows."

For long minutes, Sybil Healy continued to whisper in the fragrant darkness. All about them hung her clothing scented with lavender. If one moved, their silken rustle whispered in the air. Sybil leaned close to Wentworth. She laughed softly. "Is this a trick, sir, to get us alone?" Her shoulder pressed against his chest, her head was tilted up and back so that he looked down into the pale nearness of her face. Her lips were apart....

Wentworth spoke with weary disinterest. "There is a person coming here tonight to kill you. As long as that person remains alive and at large, your life will be in danger. If you don't remain quiet, the murderer will not come in." He put his hand on her shoulder, and startlingly his fingers touched not silk, but warm bare flesh. He merely pushed gently until she was standing straight instead of leaning against him. "If you don't mind, Mrs. Healy," he said, "I'm quite fatigued."

HER SHOULDER jerked away from his hand with a rustle

of the silks that hung close about them, and for long moments more she stood stiffly.

"I'm growing tired of this," she said in a normal speaking tone, uglily.

Wentworth slapped a hand over her mouth. "Silent!" he hissed in her ear. "Look!"

He pointed across the room with a rigid arm that showed blackly against the rosy cone of light beside the bed. Beyond that cone was darkness that was impenetrable, but in that darkness something without form or character moved. Beneath his imprisoning hands, Wentworth felt the woman become rigid. He released her gently, taking her wrist, and she stood unmoving, her breath shallow and light. His hand felt the heavy pounding of the pulse in her arm.

Slowly the movement drew nearer the bed. Wentworth felt excitement mount in his own breast. He kept his eyes on the farthest dim edge of that cone of soft light. Into that peripheral where the rose merged with gray and black, where it laid an indefinite ray upon the soft rug, a foot showed. It wore a gleaming patent leather shoe and from it rose a black trouser leg. The other foot thrust forward softly and a man stood beside the bed.

The breath of the woman beside Wentworth grew so labored that he was forced to squeeze her wrist in warning. She silenced herself. Stealthily the man's hands slipped forward into the light. In the right hand, poised with thumb upon the plunger, he held a hypodermic needle. But the man's face was still in darkness. It was possible to see only that he was tall and thin....

His hands began to ease aside the silken coverlets of the bed, the needle slid forward….

Wentworth pressed a flash light into Sybil Healy's hand.

"I have a gun," he whispered, "go ahead!"

Her breath caught in her throat, eased out hissingly so that Wentworth knew her teeth were clamped tightly. She swayed forward from beside him. Light streamed from the torch. A man's face twisted up whitely above the bed, a man's face with a small puckery mouth, but handsome nevertheless, the face of Heinrich Scarlet!

"So nice of you, dear," Sybil's voice purred, "to pay me a visit. What is that dear little toy in your hand?"

She strolled toward the foot of the bed, entirely self-possessed. Wentworth saw her outlined against the glare of the hand torch, the svelte matured lines of her figure plainly visible through the scanty robes.

"Ah, darling," said Scarlet, straightening, wiping the moment's fright from his face. "I was just going to surprise you.

"Surprise me, hell!" Sybil Healy spat out. *That needle holds hydrophobia germs!*"

Scarlet's words jerked out, "Shut up, you fool!"

Sybil threw back her head and laughed wildly once. "Fool, is it!" Words poured out now. "Fool, is it! I've given up everything for you, helped you kill my husband, helped you fool the world into thinking Douglas Brent was a polished gentleman named Heinrich Scarlet, helped you to hide safely here while your mad dogs threw the wealth of the country into Bert's lap, so when he was dead and we were married…."

THE MAN sprang around the foot of the bed.

"Get back, or I'll shoot," Sybil hit out at him and there was no softness in her voice. Scarlet halted, but his voice was swift and urgent.

"Honest, darling," he said, "this needle had only narcotics in it. I've got to remove that fellow Wentworth tonight and I wanted you to have an unshakable alibi. Wentworth is suspicious somehow. That's why he's hanging around. His order to arrest Healy was a blind…."

Sybil laughed again and it was a hateful sound. "I know how much you want to shield me, you coward. You wanted me to kill my own husband! I see now that you planned for me to be revealed as his murderer!"

"But darling, all this is ridiculous," Scarlet cut in. "I couldn't possibly get any of the money *unless I married you!*"

Silence fell between them, silence and uncertainty. Sybil was wavering between what she wanted to believe and the evidence of her senses.

"Remember the walk in the garden," Wentworth spoke in to the silence calmly. Scarlet let out a small, startled cry.

"Stand still, Scarlet. My gun is pointed at your heart!" Wentworth snapped, went on with coldly precise syllables. "The walk in the garden, Mrs. Healy, when Scarlet killed a wolf he knew was there, when he comforted Doris in his arms. *Wasn't Doris yours and Healy's sole heir, Mrs. Healy?*"

Sybil gasped. "Doris! You planned to kill me and marry Doris! That was why you had me make a will in her favor.

You said it would divert suspicion from me."

She took a quick, stride forward and struck viciously at Scarlet's face with the flashlight. The glass smashed and they were in darkness. Scarlet let out a choked shout, hoarse and frightened, and reeled backward. Wentworth crossed toward him in a swift bound. A gun blasted. Wentworth felt the burning hammer blow of the bullet against his chest. He reeled against the bed and, bracing, yanked out his gun. Scarlet's silhouette raced toward the window.

Coolly Wentworth squeezed the trigger. Scarlet stumbled. Again and again Wentworth fired until he had emptied the last bullet into that sagging body.

Reeling, weak from the hot pain of the wound in his chest, Wentworth moved heavily forward until he stood over the thin man on the floor, the thin man flat on his back on the floor with six bullets in his vitals, with his hands flung wide and his bony face turned upward.

The Spider threw back his head and laughed a little wildly.

"Master of the Hordes!" he cried. "Who's master now?"

He laughed again and his knees gave way and he slumped unconscious to the ground.

CHAPTER 23
CATHARSIS

THE WORLD had to wait two weeks for the solution of the riddle of the Mad Hordes, two weeks while Wentworth tossed in pain upon a bed of fever from the wound of a poisoned bullet, two weeks in which Sybil Healy and Scarlet died in their cells of hydrophobia—Scarlet had pricked her with the needle during their struggle—two weeks in which Nita Van Sloan was ceaselessly beside him.

But finally the fever lifted and Wentworth, pale, but strengthening daily, was able to give his story to the high army officials and government dignitaries who waited upon him.

"Briefly the answer is this," Wentworth told them. "When the crimes pointed toward Brent, I put a watch over every man in any way connected with Healy who could fit with the general description of Brent, which meant a thin, tall man and that was about all. I found greasepaint in a headquarters of the Hordes and that pointed to disguise.

"Scarlet obviously was involved with Sybil Healy, perhaps with the daughter, the only means through which any one could profit by the destruction of Healy's business and industrial rivals…."

"But you insisted on Healy's arrest," a short, worried man with a perpetual frown broke in—one of the best criminal prosecutors in the government's many starred bureaus.

"Certainly," said Wentworth, "that was the only sure way I had to protect him from murder, and his murder was inevitable if these men were to profit. I was not sure of my criminal, I had no evidence against him. So I moved to defend the victim. The stubbornness of the police defeated me there."

HE STARED moodily at the white wall opposite, traced circles on the counterpane with a finger still brown and strong, though it seemed fragilely thin.

"As I said, I had no evidence that would stand up in courts," he resumed. "I must trap the suspects. Mrs. Healy obviously had expected to marry Scarlet. From the course of events, he just as obviously expected to marry the daughter.

"You've got Scarlet's and Mrs. Healy's dialogue over the dictograph I rigged there. It was a full confession."

The worried man still frowned. "But I don't understand your earlier reference to greasepaint as the clue."

Wentworth frowned. He was tired. Nita put an anxious hand on his head and felt the dry heat of fever. "I think, gentlemen, that you'd better postpone this," she said.

Wentworth shook his head slowly, smiling into her blue eyes.

"Just one minute more, darling," he said. He turned to the worried small man. "Healy knew Brent. I knew that. Hence greasepaint—and other make-up materials—were the key to the whole case." He smiled wearily at the men. "I bid you gentlemen good day, I've got a lot of sleep to catch up on."

www.ingramcontent.com/pod-product-compliance
Lightning Source LLC
Chambersburg PA
CBHW020438180626
46812CB00003B/1301